MATED IN MIST

A TALON PACK NOVEL

CARRIE ANN RYAN

Mated in Mist
A Talon Pack Novel

By
Carrie Ann Ryan

COPYRIGHT

Mated in Mist
A Talon Pack Novel
By: Carrie Ann Ryan
© 2016 Carrie Ann Ryan

For more information, please join Carrie Ann Ryan's
To interact with Carrie Ann Ryan, you can join her

PRAISE FOR CARRIE ANN RYAN.... PRAISE FOR CARRIE ANN RYAN

"Carrie Ann Ryan knows how to pull your heartstrings and make your pulse pound! Her wonderful Redwood Pack series will draw you in and keep you reading long into the night. I can't wait to see what comes next with the new generation, the Talons. Keep them coming, Carrie Ann!" – Lara Adrian, New York Times bestselling author of CRAVE THE NIGHT

"Carrie Ann Ryan never fails to draw readers in with passion, raw sensuality, and characters that pop off the page. Any book by Carrie Ann is an absolute treat." – New York Times Bestselling Author J. Kenner

"With snarky humor, sizzling love scenes, and brilliant, imaginative worldbuilding, The Dante's Circle series reads as if Carrie Ann Ryan peeked at my personal wish list!" – NYT Bestselling Author, Larissa Ione

"Carrie Ann Ryan writes sexy shifters in a world full of

passionate happily-ever-afters." – New York Times Best-selling Author Vivian Arend

"Carrie Ann's books are sexy with characters you can't help but love from page one. They are heat and heart blended to perfection." New York Times Bestselling Author Jayne Rylon

Carrie Ann Ryan's books are wickedly funny and deliciously hot, with plenty of twists to keep you guessing. They'll keep you up all night!" USA Today Bestselling Author Cari Quinn

"Once again, Carrie Ann Ryan knocks the Dante's Circle series out of the park. The queen of hot, sexy, enthralling paranormal romance, Carrie Ann is an author not to miss!" New York Times bestselling Author Marie Harte

Praise for the Redwood Pack Series...

"You will not be disappointed in the Redwood Pack." Books-n-Kisses

"I was so completely immersed in this story that I felt what the characters felt. BLOWN AWAY." Delphina's Book Reviews.

"I love all the wolves in the Redwood Pack and eagerly anticipate all the brothers' stories." The Book Vixen

"Shifter romances are a dime a dozen, but good ones aren't as plentiful as one would think. This is one of the goods one." Book Binge

"With the hints of things to come for the Redwoods, I can't wait to read the next book!" Scorching Book Reviews

"Ryan outdid herself on this book." The Romance Reviews

Praise for the Dante's Circle Series...

"This author better write the next books quickly or I will Occupy Her Lawn until she releases more! Pure romance enjoyment here. Now go put this on your TBR pile—shoo!" The Book Vixen

"I, for one, will definitely be following the series to see what happens to the seven." Cocktails & Books

"The world of Dante's Circle series is enthralling and with each book gets deeper and deeper as does Carrie Ann's writing." Literal Addiction

Praise for the Montgomery Ink Series...

"Shea and Shep are so cute together and really offset each other in a brilliant way. " Literal Addiction

"This was a very quick and spicy read. I really enjoyed reading about Sassy, Rafe & Ian. I really hope there will be more of these three in the future." Books n Kisses

Praise for the Holiday, Montana Series...

"Charmed Spirits was a solid first book in this new series and I'm looking forward to seeing where it goes." RR@H Novel Thoughts & Book Thoughts

"If you're looking for a light book full of magic, love and hot little scenes on various objects, then this book is for you!

You'll soon find that tables are no longer for eating meals of the food variety ... Bon appétit!" Under the Covers

"The book was well written and had the perfect setting the steamy bits where really really hot and the story one of sweet romance. Well done Carrie" Bitten by Love Reviews

DEDICATION

To my readers.
You're the reason I do this.

ACKNOWLEDGMENTS

Another book, another team that I adore. I so enjoyed diving deep into Ryder and Leah's story and I know I couldn't have done it without a few people. Thank you Chelle for not only editing my book, but also plotting with me. You totally helped me break through a Leah's inner shields. I feel like Leah has a little part of each of us and that makes me so happy.

Thank you to the rest of me team—Charity, Stephanie, and Dr. Hubby. Y'all help me with so many things with each book. I know I couldn't do it without any of you.

I love my wolves. The Redwood Pack was the first series I ever wrote and now I get to write the next generation with the Talon Pack. I am truly blessed. Thank you dear readers for loving my books. Thank you for sharing my posts, buying my books, and telling your friends.

You guys are amazing!

MATED IN MIST MATED IN MIST

As Heir to the Talon Pack, Ryder Brentwood carries the responsibility of not only protecting his Pack, but ensuring its future. Only no one knows that as he does this, he must also shield his people from their past. When a witch with no ties bursts into his life, he must decide if he can overcome the depravity of his secrets and trust the one person who could break the fragile hold on his control.

Grieving over the loss of her twin and on the run from the unknown, Leah Helm knows she is far more alone than she thought possible. Her coven shunned her before she was born and the wolves she sought protection with are in a war of their own. When a wolf with a whisper of secrets is forced to work with her in order to protect their people, she finds she might not be so alone after all.

The world knows more than they ever have before about those shrouded in darkness, while Ryder and Leah are thrust into the center of a conflict they never should have been part of to begin with. On their journey they must not only fight those against them, but the burning temptation that is flaring between them. Fate might have paved their path, but that doesn't mean they have to follow.

CHAPTER
ONE

Death followed them, hunted them, craved them. It would not win. It couldn't.

Leah Helm pushed her body to the limit, her chest heaving as she ran. She could hear the others following her, trying to catch her and Roland. Only the goddess knew why. She might not have the extrasensory abilities of the wolves that lived nearby, but the monsters that had her and her brother on the run weren't even bothering to be quiet.

Apparently, their pursuers thought there was no need to be silent on their hunt. They thought they'd catch her and Roland easily. Catch or kill, she wasn't sure. Either way, it wasn't something Leah could deal with right then. Or deal with ever.

Her lungs burned and she desperately needed water. She was a reasonably strong water witch, but even she couldn't suck the water from the air to drink or use. Her twin couldn't either, though they each had their own strengths when it came to their powers. Leah didn't want to have to find out if each of them had enough within themselves to defeat those following them.

She was too afraid it wouldn't be enough.

Roland gripped her hand and tugged her toward a group of trees. The branches were full, creating a sort of cover with their leaves, though she knew it wouldn't be enough. She followed him, her legs all but giving out from the exertion. When she spotted a cave, she could have wept. It was off the beaten path, and if they were careful covering their tracks, they could rest there for a few moments. At least, that's what she hoped her twin was thinking. As they usually thought along the same lines, there was a good chance of that.

He pulled her toward the opening and ducked beneath the lower rocks. She followed, her heart beating erratically and her tongue so dry she knew she wouldn't be able to spell a single thing until she got some water in her system. Roland turned and pushed her through before following and using what had to be the last of his magic to cover their tracks. He practically slumped over after the effort, yet he pushed her hands away when she tried to help him.

Her body shook and she took a good look at herself before continuing on, praying there was another way out of the cave. If not, they might be trapped.

Dirt and blood covered her jeans from where she'd fallen and scraped her knees. It hadn't stung until she looked down and noticed. Now it throbbed, along with every other ache and pain in her body. She felt like she was an old woman with the joints to match, rather than the twenty-nine-year-old she was.

Of course, with the way she'd been forced to live her life thus far, she wasn't sure she'd ever felt her age.

"Come on," Roland whispered once they were far enough inside the cave that she couldn't hear their pursuers anymore. That could be a good thing—or a very, very bad one. "I sense a pond or a decent body of water within the cave. Don't you?"

She didn't sense anything, but that was because she couldn't see past the fear. And that was deadly. She was smarter than this—she'd had to be in order to survive this long.

Leah took a deep breath and her eyes widened as the scent of pure water touched her tongue. Her body almost shivered in pure delight. While most witches didn't need their actual element around them to be able to practice, being cut off from it for so long made it almost impossible to spell or protect oneself. As a water witch, she needed water to feel whole. Earth witches didn't like to be parted from nature for too long, and fire witches liked warmth. Though, with fire witches, their element was connected to their emotions a little more tightly, and they used their powers differently. Air witches had it a little easier when it came to finding their element, but they had their own issues when it came to their powers. And spirit witches...well, she wasn't sure what they needed. And she honestly didn't want to know. Most of them scared her.

Usually, Leah only needed to drink a glass of water a day

to be fine spell-wise, and since most people drank more than that, it wasn't a problem.

However, she and Roland had been running for days from those who wanted to hurt them, and it had been an oddly dry week in the Pacific Northwest. They'd lost their packs with their water bottles when one of the humans on their tail had gotten far too close, and it hadn't rained more than that morning's sprinkle in days.

Her body was starving for food, water, rest, and care.

They crawled through the narrow tunnel toward the scent of water and she almost fell to her chest at the sight of a clear pool surrounded by crystals and different rock formations. Stalactites and stalagmites jetted from the rock, and she wanted to weep at its beauty.

"Sweet goddess, it's glorious," Roland whispered then smiled over his shoulder at her.

It went straight to her heart. It wasn't his old smile—the one that told her that everything would be okay. No, this one held the pain and strain of running for so long. First from those who should have opened their arms to them, then from those who would see them dead rather than find out who they truly were.

The humans who wanted her people dead.

Only, she couldn't fight them to protect herself because not all humans knew witches were real. Instead, they thought witches were from movies or were a weird cult that spent the nights dancing naked in the moonlight and drawing pentagrams in dirt.

She rarely danced in the moonlight.

And she'd never done it naked.

But those who followed them with guns and traps knew Roland and Leah were witches. And that scared her. The wolves were the ones out of hiding—not her people. The Packs had been forced into the open, and now their very lives and way of life were on the line. Leah had never wanted that for the witches—even if the covens had never wanted her family to be part of their inner circles.

Her mind and her heart hurt from thinking about that so she pushed it aside for the moment and crawled the last few feet to the side of the pool. As soon as her hand touched the top of the water, her whole body shuddered in bliss. The pores of her skin opened, beckoning the sweet glory of her powers. She'd never been this dry before in her life, and she knew her brother hadn't been either.

It had been dangerous for both of them.

With her senses alert in case the humans found them within the cave, she brought her cupped hand to her lips and drank. Her parched tongue lapped it up and she swallowed as much as she could without choking. It tasted of the heavens and the goddess's blessings. She drank until she couldn't fit any more in her stomach then finally wiped her face, her hands still shaking and her heart beating too fast. But she could breathe again.

That had to count for something.

"You're bleeding, little sister," Roland said, bringing her out of her thoughts.

She blinked up at him; aware he'd also washed the grime off his face. "I know," she whispered, her voice still a bit hoarse from lack of use.

"Do you want me to heal you, or do you want to do it yourself?"

She shook her head and held out a hand. He gripped it firmly and her soul settled. They were twins, witches, and best friends. She didn't know what she'd do without him.

"I can heal myself. Check yourself for wounds and heal, as well." She pressed her lips together and searched around the small cave that was their refuge for the time being. "We can't stay here for too much longer."

Roland scowled. "I know. I hate this. We just need to get a bit closer and then we might be okay."

She frowned. "Closer to what? Why won't you tell me where we're going?" She didn't like this. They usually made plans together, but he, apparently, had an idea and refused to tell her. "What if we become separated and we need to meet up?"

"Then let's not become separated. We're almost there, little sister. Just believe."

She wasn't sure what to believe in right then. If he wasn't telling her where they were going, then it must mean she wasn't going to like the destination. But still, she should be told. Needed to be prepared. Anyplace had to be better than the middle of nowhere on the run from humans who wanted her head.

But once Roland set his mind on something, there was no way she could stop him.

Instead of asking again, though, she went about healing her wounds, gently placing her hands on her knees and chanting softly. The water in her system touched her soul and ignited the power the goddess had blessed her with.

She wasn't a true Healer like the wolves had, but she had enough power within her to heal at least somewhat. It was a maternal family trait within her witch line.

The sharp pain in her knees eased into a dull throb and she stopped, not wanting to use too much power in case they needed to use it again later. Not that she was sure she could use magic out in the open. There were always eyes on them.

Always.

Roland worked on his cuts and scrapes, his magic a warm pulse against her own. She looked up to ask about the next step in the plan, then found her face pressed against the rocks, her twin's body covering hers, a cacophony filling the air.

Rock shattered around them as the humans kept shooting. Since there was a ridge of rocks between the humans and her brother and her, there was a slight chance they might make it out of this alive. Sharp rocks exploded in front of her as the enemy shot again and she had to duck to avoid flying shards. Thankfully, the angle between her and the one shooting at her wasn't the greatest, so she and Roland had a small window of time where they could escape. At least, that's what she hoped.

Her brother pulled her up, and they scooted to the side, using a lower rock formation for cover.

"When I say go, run, crawl, do anything to get out. You hear me?" Roland's voice held an edge of fear she hadn't heard from him before, and she gripped his arm.

"Don't you dare play hero. We'll get out of this together."

He kissed her forehead and nodded. "I promise, little

sister, I'm not leaving this world anytime soon." He held out his hands, and she reached out to grip his arms.

"Roland! They might have cameras! They did before. You can't use magic."

He raised his chin and looked over his shoulder at her. "Maybe it's time to fight for our lives, rather than protect a group of people who've never wanted us."

Her heart ached, but she couldn't stop him, not when he was like this. If the cameras and surveillance equipment were there and they caught Roland using magic, all might be lost. Or maybe these humans only had guns and bullets.

When had she started hoping for merely guns in the hands of the enemy?

What had her life become?

Magic washed over her as Roland pulled on the pool and a wave of water crashed into the humans just now crawling over the rise. They screamed, trying to fight for air, and she had to look away. With all she'd seen, all she'd been forced to do, she should have been able to deal with death or dying, but she couldn't.

Not anymore.

It was all too much.

Instead of focusing on what her brother was doing to save their lives, she did her part. She searched the edges of the pool for another tunnel or pathway, knowing going back the way they had come might be lost to them. Even if Roland dealt with those at the edge of the pool, there were most likely others at the entrance to the tunnel.

She narrowed her eyes, focusing as hard as she could.

Tendrils of sensation covered her skin and she fought

off a shudder. She hated using magic for this. She'd prefer to heal or help the earth, rather than use it to save herself.

There.

A darkened crevice that looked big enough for even Roland's broad shoulders. She pushed out with her magic, letting it dance off the water molecules in the air. Humans wouldn't be able to see this, thankfully, but she was draining what little powers she had. Fast. She did her best to settle her pulse so she could sense if the air in the tunnel was stale or not, but it was a lost cause with the screaming, the crash of water, and her brother by her side, doing what he could to save them. She couldn't concentrate properly.

Finally, when she was able to center herself enough to focus on her intent, she realized that the air tasted fresh. She could have cried, but held herself in check. She could weep when they were safe. And since she didn't know if that would ever be possible again, she would just have to hold in the tears. Forever.

"Roland!" she shouted over the din. "Come on!"

He turned to her, his eyes wide and dark, but he nodded. Hurting others hurt them. But there was no way around it; to save their lives, they had to do what they must.

She crawled around the edges of the pool as the humans who made it out of the water surge coughed and hacked. If she and Roland moved quickly enough, they could be through the crevasse and out of the cave before the humans gathered themselves.

With Roland behind her, they made it to the opening where they could stand fully. Then they ran.

"Find the fucking witches and burn them!"

She tripped over her own feet at the shout, but Roland caught her arm. She shook it off and pushed at him, trying to get him to move faster. As long as he was safe, she would be okay. She jumped over a fallen log, the bark digging into her hands as she tried not to fall flat on her face. Her feet ached and her muscles quaked and the last of her energy reserves were depleting far too quickly.

Leah ran behind her twin brother, her pulse racing in her throat. They were coming. They knew. Roland reached out behind him, and she pushed his hand away.

"Keep going. I can keep up. Don't worry about me and end up tripping yourself."

She wished she could pull on the water around them now that she had enough in her system thanks to the cave, but it was too dangerous. With those behind them and her body wearing down after running for far too long, using magic would be a death sentence.

"I'm not leaving you behind, Leah. So run your fucking ass off. There's a safe house up the road." He grinned over his shoulder, that lock of hair she loved falling over his forehead. "I'll never lead you astray, little sister."

She smiled at him despite the fact that they were both running for their lives. "You're not that much older than me, Ro."

"It's enough. Now let's go."

He turned back, only to freeze in his tracks. It took a minute for the crack in the air to register. Roland fell to his knees, and Leah screamed.

"Roland!"

She raised her hands, the water on the leaves of the

trees from that morning's rainfall rising into the air with her pain, her agony.

Another crack rent the air.

A gunshot. That's what that was.

A sizzling pain seared her side, a fiery heat that wouldn't be quenched by the water at her fingertips. She tried to breathe, only to cough, her legs going out from under her.

She fell beside her brother, her arms reaching for him, only to come up short.

Roland lay at an odd angle, his face toward her. His eyes wide, unseeing in death. While the second gunshot had hit her in the side, his had hit him directly in the chest.

Her brother, her twin, her fellow witch.

Gone.

The darkness came, and she didn't fight. She'd been running for so long, and now she had nothing left.

Only hollowness.

They had come for the witches...and they had won.

SCREAMING.

Silence.

Pain.

Numbness.

Breath.

Choking.

Drowning.

Leah couldn't drown. She was a water witch. Drowning for her would be an insult to everything she was...or was it everything she once had been?

Was she dead?

She had to be dead. She couldn't feel anything, yet could feel everything all at once. It didn't make sense. If this were hell, she didn't know how she would make it for eternity with this sense of unknowing.

Something brushed against her arm and she flinched.

Wait. She'd felt that. Felt her arm and felt herself flinch.

Maybe she was alive and merely had to open her eyes.

Never had the word merely been such a lie.

Her eyes wouldn't work. How had she opened her eyes before? Why couldn't she quite remember?

Murmurs of voices filtered in through the deafening silence and Leah froze. Or at least she thought she had. She didn't know what was what anymore.

"I think she's waking up." A deep voice.

"Will she be dangerous?" Another deep voice.

"She was all but dead when we found her. Be thankful she's alive at all." This voice was just as deep, but it hit her like a sledgehammer. Her magic perked up, reaching out toward the man who had last spoken. She didn't know why it was doing that, but just the sound of his voice let her body relax and her eyes feel lighter, not so heavy and weighed down.

"Did you see that?" The first voice asked. "Ryder, speak again. She stopped thrashing at the sound of your voice."

Ryder.

His name was Ryder.

Why was that important?

And where was she? Where was Roland? What had happened? And had she truly been thrashing?

She pried her eyes open and promptly shut them at the bright light overhead.

"Turn down the lights, Walker," Ryder ordered.

Someone touched her hand, and her eyes shot open again. Three bearded men stood over her, gruff looking and scary as hell. She did what any sane woman would do. She shot out her fist, knocked one of them on the chin, then rolled off the bed. They would not have her. They would not dissect her or study her. Use her. The humans chasing her might have called for her death, but if she was now with them, alive and captive, she didn't want to know what "studies" they were planning. She'd heard the rumors, heard of the nightmares. She would not give in.

Her chest ached and her side burned something fierce, but she ignored it. Instead, she grabbed the scissors that lay on the counter beside the medical bed she'd woken up on.

One of the men blocked the door while the other rubbed his chin. The third moved toward her, hands out. She put her back to the wall, aware there wasn't another way out of the room except her death.

But she wouldn't kill herself.

Not if there was any fight left in her. As a water witch, she may not be inherently violent, but the will to live was stronger than she'd thought. After all that had happened... she still fought.

"It's okay," the one with his hands out said. "It's going to be okay."

She remembered that voice. This one was Ryder. Her inner witch pulsated at his voice, but she pushed that away, not understanding.

She licked her lips but didn't lower the scissors. "You can't have me. I won't let you kill me."

Ryder tilted his head, reminding her of a dog or cat. "Why would you think we would hurt you, little one?"

She narrowed her eyes at the term. "You took me to this...place, and now I'm in a medical room with three men I don't know. I remember you following me, trying to kill me. I remember..." she trailed off. Her throat ached from speaking, but that was not why she'd stopped talking.

Flashes of memory came at her and she tried to make sense of it all. She'd been running from humans out to get her. She remembered that. But what else? What else had happened? Something sparked just out of reach within her mind, and she lost the fragment as quickly as it had appeared.

"We weren't the ones chasing you," the one rubbing his jaw said gruffly. "I'm Gideon, Alpha of the Talon Pack. We're wolves. Not the humans who were out for you."

Wait. Wolves? Would they try to rip her to shreds like the people who watched too many movies thought? Or were they like her, forced to live in secret for so long that no one truly understood? Unlike other witches, she hadn't known wolves in person so she didn't know how they worked. She only knew to keep hidden was to keep safe.

She frowned, her hand lowering somewhat. She'd just hit the Alpha of the Talon Pack. That probably wasn't the smartest thing to do, but she hadn't known at the time.

"If you're wolves, then why do you have me here?" She let her eyes rest on the one they called Ryder, and her magic settled over her, wanting to know more.

"You don't remember?" Ryder asked. "You were shot. What's your name? We found you and another witch in the woods. What was he to you?" He blinked, as if he hadn't meant to say that part, but Leah didn't care.

Instead, she dropped the weapon from her hand and let out a keening wail.

"No, no, no, no, no." She shook her head and let her hands come up to her mouth. "No, no, no."

Ryder knelt in front of her and pushed the scissors across the floor to where Gideon stopped them with his boot. But she couldn't care about that. She couldn't care about anything.

"Roland..." she choked out a breath. "Roland."

"Who is Roland?" Ryder asked, his hand outstretched. When he brushed her shoulder, she didn't pull back. Instead, she leaned in to his touch. The move seemed to surprise both of them.

"My br-brother." She hiccupped a sob. "I'm...I'm Leah. Roland is...was my brother." Tears fell and she tried to suck in breath, but her lungs weren't working. "They killed him. They shot him right in front of me." Her hand went to her side and she winced.

Ryder scooted closer and let his hand cover hers along her side. "They shot you too, Leah."

"He's gone?" she asked, the blessed numbness not coming back. Instead, all she felt was the agony she couldn't ignore.

At Ryder's nod, she let herself fall apart. There wasn't a reason to be strong anymore.

Roland was gone.

He was the best of them, the one that should have made it. She was just Leah, witch with no home, no family.

She was alone.

Forever.

And with that thought, her soul shattered into a million pieces. She cried and let the tears wash over her, the magic within the water falling from her body, her entire being aching in sorrow. She barely noticed the strong arms wrapping around her, barely noticed the scent of wolf and man settling over her as she wept.

Wept for the injustice, wept for her brother.

Wept for herself.

Because now, she had no reason to keep running, no place to run to.

She was Leah Helm, water witch with no coven.

And nothing more.

CHAPTER
TWO

Ryder Brentwood stared down at the small woman in his arms and tried to keep his wolf from taking control. His inner beast rubbed against his skin, pushing at him to do more than merely cradle the sobbing woman. His wolf wanted to rip anyone who had ever hurt her to shreds. It wanted to take her away from the prying eyes of his brothers and keep her safe and warm in his home. It wanted to tend to her wounds and wait for her to be healthy again so he could slide deep into her warm heat and call her his for all time.

What the ever-loving hell?

Ryder didn't have time for his wolf to go batshit crazy over a woman they didn't know. And he sure as hell didn't have time for this mating business. He pushed those thoughts to the side and promised his wolf he'd deal with them later.

Or not at all.

Leah gripped his shirt, tugging him closer, and he did the only thing he could do at the moment. He shifted slightly so he could gather her more firmly in his arms and therefore his lap. She curled into him, and he had a feeling she had no idea she was even doing it. Her eyes were closed, and her tears soaked his shirt. At that moment, he was just a warm body for her to grieve onto, to hold onto in the darkest of times. His heart raced, but he did his best to calm it. Her ear was right over his chest, and he knew she could feel the now-steady thump against her cheek. If his wolf could give that to her, then Ryder would, as well. It was the least he could do during her time of grief.

Of course, the fact that he couldn't seem to keep his hand out of her soft, honey-brown hair was another matter. Though it looked as if she had been on the run for far too long and hadn't been able to fully clean it, the strands still felt soft to his touch. It was long, thick, and straight. He could imagine it spread over her pillow as she slept, or even brushing along his skin as they came together.

No, he couldn't imagine that. Because he wouldn't be imagining that.

She let out a whimper and he tucked her closer. He pressed his cheek to the top of her head, letting her know he was there. She might be a witch, but he was a wolf. Wolves were tactile creatures and needed touch to survive. He'd known a few wolves who'd gone touch-starved in the past under his father's reign as Alpha. Ryder, as the Heir, would never let that happen. Not while he drew breath.

Again, he pushed the thoughts of his past and whatever future he didn't want to think about out of his head. The only thing that mattered at the moment was Leah and her pain. It overwhelmed him, as did the power he felt running through her veins. He'd met a few witches in his time—he was over a century old—but he'd never held one so close. He'd hugged his friend Quinn's mate Gina before, but it hadn't been for long. As Quinn would readily tear off Ryder's face for daring to touch her for more than a moment, Ryder understood. Mating was something precious.

Mating was something he would never have.

He closed his eyes, pushing those thoughts from his brain once again. He needed to focus, needed to worry about the here and now—not what would never be.

Gina was a fire witch. Or, half-witch, at least. Her birth mother had been a witch and her birth father a wolf. So when Ryder hugged her, he felt the crackle of her energy. The former Redwood Pack Healer was an earth witch; her energy was a little more grounded.

But Leah? Hers was a rush of cool power, flowing over him, under him, through him. And with how weak she was, he knew this wasn't her at peak energy level. He couldn't wait to see her at full strength.

He sniffed, frowned at the coppery scent of blood in the air.

His gaze shot to his brother, Walker, their Healer.

Walker, one of the triplets, knelt beside Ryder and Leah with a needle in his hand. "She's not Pack so my powers won't do her much good," his brother explained, his voice a low drawl. "If she keeps moving like that, she's going to tear her wound right open again." Walker inhaled deeply. "Or she may have already. It doesn't smell like she did it too badly, but if we don't keep her still, it's just going to get worse."

Ryder nodded, understanding. Leah whimpered again, and he ran a hand over her arm. "Leah, keep still, you're hurting yourself." He kept his voice light, but the order was there.

She kept crying, her hands digging into his shirt.

Walker let out a sigh then injected her with the needle. Leah winced in Ryder's arms and he did his best to soothe her. When she stopped moving and her breath came in an even rhythm, Ryder leaned back against the wall.

"Let me take her and put her back on the bed," Walker said softly.

"Then we can talk about what comes next," Gideon, his brother, the Alpha, put in. Gideon had been on the sidelines for most of the encounter, watching with a careful eye as Ryder had done his best to calm and comfort Leah.

"I've got her," Ryder said without thinking. He should have let Walker take her and walk away, but he couldn't. Instead, he got curious looks from both of his brothers and a knowing gleam, as well.

He ignored them and used the wall to help him stand with Leah in his arms. He could have done it easily just by using the strength in his thighs, but he hadn't wanted to jostle her too much. She was already in enough pain as it was.

He couldn't imagine her agony.

Ryder set her down on the bed and kept ahold of her hand, even though he knew he should let her go. Walker got to work on her gunshot wound while Gideon stood silently by, his arms crossed over his chest.

Ryder slowly let her hand go and took a step back. His wolf immediately revolted, ramming into him and scraping its claws on the underside of his skin. Ryder took a deep breath, taking control back from his wolf. Despite the fact that his claws threatened to break through the skin of his fingertips, he forced himself to be calm.

He didn't understand his reaction to this woman—or perhaps he just didn't want to.

"We need a family meeting to talk about what happened," Gideon uttered into the quiet. "We might need a Pack circle, as well, but a family meeting for now."

Ryder nodded. "I'll round up the troops." With that, he left his brothers behind so he could go find the others.

His sister Brynn would be close, he knew. She and her mate, Finn, the Heir of the Redwood Pack, had been the ones to find Leah and her brother. They'd wanted to stay and see the outcome, but neither of them had slept much. They'd been on a hunt with the Redwoods and had heard the gunshots outside the wards. Though the two dens weren't too close distance-wise, they now shared a border with a tiny strip of neutral land between them at certain points. The gunshots had happened there.

So, Finn and Brynn had run to the closest Healer.

That happened to be the Talons.

It was odd to think that two Packs could work so closely

together, but after over thirty years of finding ways to work as one without creating a single Pack, the Talons and Redwoods were finding their way. It had all started when Ryder's father, the former Alpha, had died by Gideon's hand. Ryder would have killed the bastard himself, but it had been Gideon's right to do it.

The Brentwood family had been born in agony and honed in fire. They'd suffered at the hands of their father and uncles more than anyone knew. But they were strong now. Or, at least, that's what they told themselves.

What Ryder told himself.

While that had been happening, the Redwoods had been fighting a war themselves. Only instead of fighting within, they'd been dealing with another Pack that had gone dark. Way dark. Ryder and his brothers had battled alongside the Redwoods in the end and had formed a truce, and, eventually, friendship.

It had taken another fifteen years for members to start feeling as if they could trust freely, and another fifteen years after that for their Packs to become as close to a single unit as possible. Gideon had married a Redwood Pack princess, and now, Ryder's Alpha female was a young, submissive wolf with Redwood parents and the softest smile he'd ever seen.

They were growing, settling, healing.

Of course, the world had gone to shit yet again when the humans found out about the existence of wolves. Ryder had known it would only be a matter of time before technology became too great for non-humans like him to hide anymore. Magic could only do so much, but he hadn't been prepared for the death and blood that came with the world uncovering the truth of what lay beneath the surface of their truth.

Their losses had been small so far, but he knew it wouldn't last.

It had been a year since his people were revealed, and just recently, human hate groups had begun to kill those they were afraid of. Now, politicians in Washington were debating his Pack's future without consulting them.

There was even a politician named McMaster who had called out the wolves as not being part of the human population. He hadn't called for war, but it had been damn close.

Ryder's Pack, as well as the Redwoods, were trying to figure out what to do about it. They not only needed to keep their people safe, they needed to protect the other Packs in the world, as well. The problem was much bigger than them, and at times, it seemed insurmountable.

Ryder ran a hand over his face as he made his way through the den, nodding at the few members he passed along the way. Now, they had Leah and whatever problems she'd brought with her to add to the pile. Finn and Brynn had a feeling that Leah and her brother had been running to the Pack for protection, or at least running for something. His family wouldn't turn away a person in need, even if she wasn't Pack. They weren't callous, but they would protect their Pack with everything they had.

Only he didn't know how he was going to do that.

"Ryder?"

He froze at the sound of Brynn's voice, then shook his head, trying to clear his thoughts. He'd been so stuck in his own mind, he'd almost passed Brynn's place. Or rather, her old place. He guessed she was living with the Redwoods now, with her new mate. He wasn't sure what they'd do with her place since it was mostly empty except for a few pieces of furniture. With the Pack on lockdown behind the wards thanks to the hate crimes and the uncertainty of their future, space was hard to come by. He was sure Mitchell, his cousin and Beta of the Pack, had a plan. That was his job, after all—to take care of the daily needs of the Pack while Gideon and Ryder dealt with the more harrowing jobs.

Though it seemed like Gideon was the one doing that more recently, with Ryder standing behind, trying to figure it all out.

You're nothing. Nothing. Just a waste of space. Not a true Heir.

He pushed aside the familiar diatribe echoing in his head. He didn't have time for that; didn't have time for anything.

"Sorry, Brynn," Ryder finally said as he turned to face his sister fully. "Too much going on in my head."

She studied his face, seemed to see far more than she should have. "Is it the girl? Is she okay?"

His wolf nudged him at the mention of Leah, but again, he ignored it. "She's fine." At least, he hoped she'd be. He wasn't sure if anyone could ever be fine after that.

He looked over his shoulder as people slowed to over-hear their conversation. While the others of the Pack would know about Leah soon enough, he needed to make

26

sure his family was kept up-to-date first, before there was an issue.

"Gideon wants a family meeting," he said before he said too much more.

Brynn nodded with understanding. "Gideon and Brie's place?"

"As always." With that, he turned and made his way to the Alpha's home, messaging the others as he did. For some reason, he'd wanted to tell Brynn beforehand—probably because she'd been the one to find Leah in the first place.

Brie was already at the front door when he made it to the porch, her arms wide. He let her wrap herself around him and he tugged her close for a hug. There wasn't anything sexual about it; this was his brother's mate and his wolf's Alpha. But even with all of that, it was her submissive nature that his wolf needed more than anything right then. Her wolf soothed the beast, reaching out to comfort while others needed to protect. She was perfect for the highly dominant Gideon, even if it hadn't seemed so at first.

"I have food on the table and drinks are in the fridge," Brie said into his chest.

Ryder kissed the top of her head and let her go. "Just because you're the Alpha's wife, doesn't mean you have to cook for us."

She rolled her eyes and patted him on his stomach. "I didn't. It's leftovers from one of the maternals. I was working with the other submissives today and didn't have time to cook. But since I made it home first, I figured I'd set out a spread. I'm not the baker my mother is, so it takes me extra time to make it as good as I want it."

"You're a bad liar," Ryder said as he followed her to the large dining room. It was open to the living room so everyone could grab some food and then sink into the large cushions on the couch or armchairs and talk about what needed to come next. "You're just as good as your mother." Willow Jamenson, Brie's mother, had been a bakery owner in her human life years ago and even ran a new bakery on Redwood Pack land now. Brie had learned from her mother and treated the Talons on occasion.

Brie just shrugged and handed him a stuffed mushroom. "Eat. You look like hell." She met his eyes. "Gideon called. Told me about Leah."

He met her gaze and cooled his features.

She let out a sigh. "If you want to talk, Ryder. I'm here. I'm always here."

"Thanks for the mushroom." He stuffed it in his mouth before she could question him further. Or before he said something he didn't want to share.

The others came into the house, saving him from Brie's stare. Gideon walked in first, his attention on his mate. He wrapped an arm around her waist and lifted her off her feet, bringing his lips to hers. They kissed like no one was watching, and Ryder had to look away before even he blushed. The two had been mated a year and acted as if they had just found one another. With all the time the two spent wrapped around each other, Ryder was surprised Brie hadn't ended up pregnant yet. Though he had a feeling the two were waiting until they had more time under their belts...as well as a more definite idea of what their future would be.

The world had shifted on its axis, and Ryder wasn't sure

if bringing a baby into the world was safe. In fact, his friend Quinn and Quinn's mate Gina, the fire witch, had been mated for fifteen years and were only now thinking of having a child. They were long-lived as shifters, their bodies sharing space with the soul of a wolf. Some mated couples waited a century to have a child. They were blessed with time.

Yet cursed with it all the same...

Cursed bastard.

Again, he pushed the whisper from his thoughts. He had to in order to stay sane. Or at least as sane as he could be.

His cousins Max and Mitchell went straight for the food, their attention on each other as they continued their conversation from before. He wasn't sure what it was about, but the two were brothers and had their own connection. Max may not hold a high-ranking position like his brother Mitchell, the Beta, but he was on the council that they shared with the Redwood Pack. Even if the moon goddess hadn't blessed everyone with a sacred duty, they all had their roles nonetheless.

Brandon, Walker, and Kameron came in next. They were triplets, though fraternal. They looked alike, though, almost as if they were identical but with just a hint of uniqueness. Though they were the youngest of the Brentwoods, the goddess had touched them all. Brandon was the Omega, the one who cared for the emotional wellbeing of the Pack—his quiet and caring nature an asset for all members. Walker was the Healer and able to Heal using his powers for most Packmates' wounds. Kameron was the Enforcer and it suited his icy personality. It was his job to protect the Pack from outside forces. He could feel the threat through his Pack bonds like the rest of the goddess-touched could.

Though with the way their Pack kept battling, he wasn't sure that any one of them could do their duties to the full extent anymore. In fact, he wasn't sure if they ever had. They'd been brought into the fold much later than most Pack royalty. They'd had to kill and fight for their roles, though he knew no one had truly wanted that blood on their hands.

He let out a breath and nodded at his brothers. He needed to stop thinking about the past. Yet ever since Leah had fallen into his arms and his wolf had gotten her scent, he hadn't been able to think about much except how he'd come to be and where he had to go.

The damn witch was changing everything.

"Everyone's here, so let's get started," Gideon said as he sank into his large armchair. He pulled Brie on his lap, wrapping his hand around the back of her neck. She melted into his hold, and Ryder couldn't help but feel a bit envious of the display of affection. His brother had never been like that before, so open with his feelings, and yet the man couldn't stop touching his mate.

Ryder wondered what that felt like.

You could know if you weren't such a useless piece of shit.

He closed his eyes at the whispers. He'd heard them all his life, the voices. Only recently, it wasn't voices. Just a voice.

His uncle's voice.

He sucked in a deep breath and focused on Gideon's voice instead. His Alpha would help. He had to.

He purposely ignored Brandon's stare. His Omega brother saw too much, always had.

"How's Leah?" Brie asked as she ran a hand over her mate's thigh.

"She's stable," Walker answered. "I left her with my assistant. She should be up by tomorrow morning."

Ryder let out a breath he didn't know he'd been holding. Brandon tilted his head at him.

Damn it.

"Hopefully, she'll have answers when she wakes," Gideon said.

"You think whoever was coming for her is on their way here?" Kameron asked. "I have my men on it, just in case, as do the Redwoods."

"Good," Gideon said. "And I don't know. We're all on edge, and having a witch get shot near our borders isn't helping. The fact that her brother was killed just makes it worse." He met Ryder's eyes. "I know you and Brandon and the Redwoods are meeting with the local Coven next week and now with Leah getting shot like this...it just seems too much of a coincidence."

The Coven had asked to meet with the wolves, as witches were afraid they would be next in the public eye. Shifters and witches had always gotten along and mated when the goddess willed it, but having something formal was different. He was on the taskforce to ensure there was an open line of communication, but it hadn't officially started yet.

"I don't know if we should inform the Coven we have Leah yet," Ryder said. From the looks on others' faces, he must have surprised them. With his words or the fact that he'd actually spoken, he didn't know. He didn't speak much for a reason.

The voices would know. They would hear. They always did.

"Why?" Brynn asked. She sat next to Finn, their hands clasped. "Do you think the Coven has something to do with this? Isn't she one of theirs?"

Ryder sighed. "She said she was alone," he whispered. "I don't know if she even meant to say it aloud, but she cried it. Wouldn't someone with a coven to call home not be alone? I don't know if the Coven had anything to do with it, but I just have a feeling we should stay silent about it until Leah wakes."

Gideon nodded. "I agree." With that, his brother began the next bit of business, and Ryder kept one ear on it while he went into himself. His wolf needed to run, needed to breathe. But he couldn't do that, not with Leah so close... and he didn't know why he even thought that. Why was she so important?

His body ached. His wolf ached.

His wolf wanted her. Wanted her as his mate.

And he would never have that. He couldn't.

The voices in his head grew in number, and he barely held himself in check, barely held back the whimper. It was the voices of the dead, those who had passed, those who had left this earthly realm.

They called for him. Called for help. Called for death.

He couldn't have the witch. Not with who he was.

But maybe he could help her.

Because that's what he did.

He helped.

Nothing more.

THREE

This time when Leah woke, she didn't fight back, didn't scream at the lights overhead. Instead, she slowly opened her dry eyes and stared at the ceiling. She remembered where she was this time. She hadn't forgotten, hadn't pushed aside the pain and tried to ignore the agony that lay within.

Instead, the anguish churned inside her, an ever-present part of her soul she wasn't sure would ever fade away. She didn't know if she wanted it to. Because if she let go, if she ever thought of her life without this pain, then Roland would be gone forever.

Her side still ached, but not quite as much as it had before. She remembered the fiery pain now, the way she'd fallen. She remembered it all.

Of course, that meant she remembered the way she'd fallen into Ryder's arms and broken down. She didn't even know the man, and yet she had used him as her crutch, her salvation. She honestly wasn't sure how she felt about that.

"You're awake."

She stiffened only for a moment at the baritone voice before turning her head to look at the man sitting comfortably in a rocking chair next to the wall. He had a book in his lap and reading glasses on the tip of his nose. She didn't know if wolves truly needed reading glasses with their enhanced senses, but she had to admit, the look suited him.

"Walker, right?" she asked, her voice hoarse. She cleared her throat and licked her dry lips and tried to ignore the odd sense of disappointment she felt that it wasn't Ryder looking over her. She didn't understand her fascination with that man, and to be honest, it bothered her. She wasn't a wolf, but a witch. Witches didn't have fated mates and instant connections like shifters did. She only had her powers to tell her if she would find someone her soul could be happy with. And even then, it was on the wolf to provide the mating bond.

She coughed, this time harder and in rapid succession at the track her thoughts had taken. What the hell was wrong with her? Mates? Fate? She didn't believe in all of that, not for her. She was nothing. Just a witch with no home and not enough power since she could never fully stop to train. She was too busy running for her life. There had been nothing more, nothing less than that.

Maybe she'd hit her head when she'd been shot. That could explain the idea of mates and all the crap that had nothing to do with her swirling in her mind. Her side burned as she coughed and she put her hand over her mouth, trying to control herself.

Walker set his book on the table beside him as well as his glasses and hurried toward her. Well, if you could call the way he prowled a hurry. The man looked as if he were on a leisurely stroll, yet still moved quickly.

He held out a cup of water to her then slowly moved her hand away from her mouth. At his touch, she noticed the IV attached to her hand.

"Drink this," he drawled. "I have you on a saline drip since you needed fluids."

She greedily gulped the water down, quenching her parched throat. Her magic flexed, and she let out a sigh when she lowered the cup.

"Thank you."

He nodded and filled the cup again. "I don't know what your powers are, and I hadn't wanted to ask another witch to come in here while you were unconscious to tell me. Because of that, I couldn't give you too many pain meds, as I didn't know how it would affect you. So I'm sorry if you're hurting. I also couldn't Heal your wounds like I would if you were Pack. I don't have the bonds to work with. You did need fluids, though. So I could do that at least."

He sounded annoyed that he couldn't do more for her, and yet he'd saved her life. She wasn't sure what more he could have done under the circumstances.

She drank again, this time slower. "You did more than most would do," she finally said.

Walker tilted his head, looking so much like a wolf it

startled her. "I don't know about that. And if that's what you're thinking, perhaps you need to meet better people."

Instead of commenting on that, she went back to something he'd said earlier. "I'm a water witch." She gestured with the mug she was still holding. "So thank you for the water. You're helping more than you know." Belatedly, she worried that he'd take the water away from her, afraid of her powers like so many others had been. It wasn't that she was ultra powerful, but that she'd come from...him. Come from a place that wasn't meant to be.

But Walker didn't know that.

Nor did he take her water away. Instead, he filled her cup again and checked her IV bag. "I don't know as I've met a water witch before," he said smoothly. "I probably have, but they're rare, aren't they?"

She shook her head. "We're not as rare as air or spirit witches, but we're not as prevalent as earth and fire ones. We're sort of just...in the middle I guess."

Walker nodded then leaned against the bed. She was up on one elbow, giving her side a break. "I'm glad we found you when we did, though I'm sure as hell sorry we couldn't save your brother."

A sharp lance to her heart.

"He was my twin."

Walker cursed under his breath. "I'm sorry, Leah. Damn sorry. I'm a triplet myself. I have connections, bonds to the Pack and to my siblings, but there's something different about how it is with me, Kameron, and Brandon. So, fuck, Leah. I'm sorry."

There were three of them that looked like Walker? The

Talons were a lucky Pack. Though it was Ryder that kept coming back to her mind. She pushed it out again, knowing it wasn't worth it. She would be leaving soon, running again. Wouldn't she?

"I'm sorry, as well," a voice said from the doorway. Ryder's voice.

She turned quickly and winced when she pulled on her stitches.

Ryder came to her side, a frown on his face. "Did you hurt yourself?" His nostrils flared. "I don't smell fresh blood, so that's good."

Walker let out a snort. "Big brother over here is a little overprotective it seems. Your stitches are fine, and I would guess if I gave you a pool of water and let you chant or spell, you'd be able to finish healing at least the main parts. Right?"

She pulled her gaze from Ryder's deep blue eyes and nodded at Walker. "Yes, usually. I can't heal mortal wounds or anything too critical, but I can do some healing. Nothing like you can with your bonds to the Pack."

"Can you heal others?" Ryder asked.

Her powers flared, as if they were a separate part of her, reaching out for him. She couldn't quite understand it, nor was she sure she wanted to.

"Sometimes," she said finally. "It depends on the wound and my power reserves." She let out a sigh. "I haven't had much in the way of power for a long time." That was an understatement, but she wasn't ready to tell them everything. Though something within her told her that she could trust these two, trust the Alpha and those with them, as well. She just wasn't ready to reveal her past. She wasn't sure she'd ever be ready.

"I'm a healer more than a fighter, though. I know some of the other elemental witches out there feel the opposite, but I don't like fighting." She winced. "Sorry for coming at you with the scissors. I...I didn't wake up all there."

Walker shook his head. "If you hadn't fought back after waking up in a room with three strange men, I would have been truly surprised."

Ryder shrugged. "You didn't hurt us. We're good."

"Well, thank you."

"You need more water?" Ryder asked.

She nodded slightly, and Ryder immediately turned away from her and grabbed a large metal bowl from one of the cabinets and filled it with water. "Warm, cold, or hot matter? And is it okay in metal? Or do you need glass or stone or something?"

She smiled despite the fact that her mind was going in a thousand different directions. "Metals and water temperature don't affect my powers. But thank you for being so considerate." This was one weird conversation, and she was being too polite, but she didn't have her footing. She'd do what she could to survive.

She always did.

Walker helped her sit up, and she didn't miss the way Ryder's eyes narrowed at his brother's hand on her elbow. She ignored it and took the bowl from Ryder's hands. Their fingers brushed, and she sucked in a breath. She ignored that, as well.

When she sat the bowl between her legs on the bed, the

two men watched her with fascination as she immersed her hands, chanting under her breath. She wouldn't be able to fully heal the gunshot wound as she didn't have that kind of power, but she could speed along her recovery.

It would also help if she could place her whole body within water, submerging the wound and her head, but that would have to wait. For now, she let the magic of her people wash over her, reminding her that she had something more than breath to fight with.

When she was finished, her side ached only slightly, more like a dull throb now, and both men had wide eyes. She smiled softly and lifted her hands out of the bowl. Water slid over her skin until it absorbed into her greedy reservoirs of magic.

She'd always loved to watch that happen. Roland used to make it dance along his skin and hers to make her laugh when things were dark.

Now, she wasn't sure she could do it herself, not when it would only remind her of happier times. Though thinking of the dark as happy only depressed her so she ignored it and nodded in thanks to the two Talon wolves who watched over her.

Walker took the bowl away in silence as Ryder studied her face.

"Are you feeling better now?" he asked.

She nodded. "Immensely. Thank you." She turned to Walker as he removed her IV. "Thank you both." She swallowed hard. "I will be forever grateful to you for healing me." She pressed her lips together. "I'd like to see my brother if that's okay." She let out a shuddering breath. "And then I'll get out of your hair so you can focus on what you were doing before I fell into your lives."

"You're not leaving yet," Gideon said from the doorway.

She stiffened and looked at the Alpha wolf to her right. These damn brothers kept startling her. She'd have to be better at noticing when they were near, though they were wolves, and she didn't have the extra senses they did.

"Excuse me?" she asked.

"Oh, honey, you suck at commanding sometimes." A smaller woman walked around the large man and patted him on the ass as she walked by.

Leah raised a brow even as Ryder, Walker, and a fourth man that stood behind Gideon chuckled.

"Hi, Leah, I'm Brie. Gideon's mate." The slightly taller-than-average-sized woman held out her hand for Leah to shake. Brie only looked tiny compared to Gideon and the rest of the brothers, but the woman also had a...fragile air surrounding her that Leah couldn't quite explain.

"Uh, hi," Leah said then took Brie's hand. A sense of calm spread over her and she frowned.

Brie winced. "Sorry. I'm a submissive wolf and I can't help but want to comfort. Usually, it's just with Packmates, but sometimes, my wolf reaches out to others. Anyway, what Gideon meant was you don't have to go, and frankly, we'd like you to stay so we can figure out what happened. We haven't contacted the local Coven to tell them we have you because we wanted to wait until you were awake and all, but we can do that now if you want."

Leah held out both hands. "Please don't."

Brie's eyes widened, and the rest of the men moved around the bed to face Leah.

"Is there something we should know?" Gideon asked as he put his hands on his mate's shoulders. The large Alpha wolf looked so fierce compared to the soft Brie, and it boggled Leah's mind that an Alpha would mate with a submissive. But, it wasn't Leah's business, nor was it something she should be focusing on right then.

"I...I should just go."

Ryder gripped her wrist gently and she met his gaze. "Just tell us, Leah. We can't help you if you don't tell us. You were running from someone. Who was it? Why don't you want us to talk to the Coven? We're fighting a war on one side with the humans, but we need to know if we're fighting elsewhere, as well."

She let out a breath. "I wasn't born into a coven. Roland was all I had."

"I thought that's what you meant when you said you were alone before," Ryder said softly.

She jerked. "You heard that?" Heat slashed across her cheeks and she tried to pull away. Only, he wouldn't let her.

Brie cleared her throat. "My aunt Hannah wasn't in a coven either. She's an earth witch."

"It's not uncommon for witches to not want to join forces. We're not as...connected as wolves. We don't have bonds or the same kind of structure you do. Each coven has its own Council, and there's even a larger Council that tries its best to rule all the covens." She let out a breath. "That's actually the local Coven."

Gideon let out a little growl. "That much we know," he

said. "They tried to summon us for a meeting to discuss the Unveiling, but one does not summon a wolf."

Leah let out a snort. "I wouldn't think so. You guys tend to bite, I would think. As for the Coven? Well, they don't really care if you have claws or fangs. They don't care if someone shares their blood. The local witches, at least the ones in power, aren't used to hearing the word no. Their word is law. At least to their own ears."

Gideon tilted his head, much like his brother had earlier. "I had a feeling. We would like you to stay here, but," he looked down at his mate, "we will not force you. It's not safe out there, but if you are on the run, then we need to know what—or who—is after you."

She met the Alpha's gaze for a moment then looked away, not able to handle his dominance. She didn't think most people could. "They were humans. They knew we were witches and were trying to capture us. Kill us."

The fourth man in the room let out a slight curse. He winced then sighed. "I'm Brandon, the Omega. Hell. The humans were after you?"

She nodded at Walker's triplet brother. "Yes, they were. I don't know what they saw, but Roland had to use magic to save us." She swallowed hard. "I don't know exactly why they were after us. We've been running from them for a few weeks, and before that...well, we had to hide who we were from the witches, as well. But that...that I can't talk about." She looked at Gideon again. "I'm sorry I can't talk about it, but the most pressing thing is the humans."

Gideon let out a growl, and Ryder put his hand on her

shoulder. She immediately relaxed at his touch, even as her body heated. What the hell was wrong with her?

"We couldn't find who was after you, but we'll help you," Gideon said. "When you feel more comfortable with us, I hope you'll tell us why you were running longer. Running from the witches. But as you say, you have no home, no one to run to. Considering where we found you, I'm guessing you and your twin were running either toward us or the Redwoods. Let us offer you shelter."

Something filled her, was it relief? A sense of...hope? She wasn't sure, but she couldn't quite come up with the words she needed to say. She'd never had a true shelter. Even before the humans had hunted her and Roland, she'd always had to be careful, oh so careful, of who she was. But these wolves, wolves who knew nothing about her except what she told them, were offering her sanctuary. They had their own pains, their own battles and troubles, yet they offered their home to her.

They were nothing like the beasts those that shunned her spoke of, nothing like the animals the media tried to portray them as.

"I...I would like the time to rest."

Gideon nodded as if he'd known all along that would be her answer. "We have a few homes empty. However, we have more wolves coming in from the outside world now that they are no longer safe."

"And you don't want to waste space on someone who might not be staying for too long," she finished for him. Plus, she wasn't Pack. It would make sense that they wouldn't want her too far away from their careful watch.

That way she couldn't pry to deeply into their lives as well, since they'd be the ones watching her and not the other way around.

"She can stay with me," Ryder blurted.

She froze, then looked over at him. His eyes were wide —as were his siblings'. "Huh?"

He cleared his throat. "I have a guest room. She can stay with me. I'll make sure she doesn't get lost in the den."

That reason seemed like a stretch, but she couldn't formulate the words for why that would be a bad plan. A very bad plan.

Brandon, the Omega, stepped closer to her and studied her face. She pulled back, not knowing what he was doing. Ryder's hand on her shoulder tightened.

"I think it sounds like a good idea," Brandon said softly then stepped back.

She swallowed hard and nodded. "I don't mind. As long as I'm not in the way."

"You won't be in the way," Ryder said.

Brie looked between the two of them before smiling. There was something in that smile that scared Leah to no end. There was hope there. But there was no hope where Leah was concerned. There never had been and there never would be.

"If that's what you want," Gideon said finally. "I'd like to know more about you. In fact, since you're in my den and with my Pack, I'm going to insist on it." Ryder growled. "But first, you will heal."

His tone didn't surprise her, he was an Alpha wolf, after all, but she still didn't appreciate it. She should be grateful that they were letting her stay while she found her bearings, but she could barely think.

She needed time to process. Time to reflect. Would she be staying here for long? Or would she be running again? She didn't know, but sitting in a room with a bunch of wolves she didn't know probably wouldn't help her make that choice.

Gideon's phone buzzed in his pocket, the sound echoing in the room, and he pulled it out. He read the screen and cursed before showing it to Brie, who paled.

"Oh, dear goddess," the Alpha's mate whispered.

"What is it?" Ryder asked.

Gideon met Leah's eyes. "It seems they were filming you and Roland when they attacked."

Leah's heart raced.

"Only they showed the parts where Roland used his powers to save you and himself. Nothing about their attack on you." He paused. "The witches have officially been Unveiled."

And it was her fault.

She'd shown the world that her people exist.

Now it wasn't only the wolves who had to watch their backs; who didn't know what the future would bring. The entire witch community would have to watch their every move, as well.

And it was all her fault.

She'd broken the rules, tried to save herself, and now the world would have to deal with the consequences. It wouldn't only be the witches that would see their lives shattered. As the humans realized that more and more of what they'd thought was myth was all too real, they'd have to face not only their mortality, but also their deepest fears. The dynamics of how each race reacted and lived together would change with each breath.

And she'd unwillingly been part of that.

The Coven that rejected her had once told her mother that Leah and Roland would one day be the downfall of many. She just hadn't realized they would be right, that it would be something like this.

CHAPTER
FOUR

Ryder's wolf pressed into him, needing Leah's touch more than air. The man, however, knew better than that and refused to give in. Though the pain in Leah's scent was palpable, he wasn't about to do what his wolf wanted to do—claim her so they alone could care for her.

They sat in Walker's living room since his home was attached to the clinic. They hadn't called for the entire family to watch the footage, as they could easily watch at home, and there would be a meeting later to discuss it anyway. However, Brandon, Gideon, Brie, Walker, Leah and himself remained to watch the world change yet again.

Leah sat next to him, as his wolf wouldn't let any other arrangement work. He'd tried to keep a respectable distance between them, but then Brandon had sat on the other side of Leah, and Ryder had not so subtlety pressed his leg into hers. The others had noticed, of course, but he'd noticed the way her shoulders had lowered at his touch.

Whatever was happening between them wasn't one-sided, it seemed.

And that would only make things that much harder when the time came to do what must be done.

"As you can see, witches are real," the newscaster was saying, bringing Ryder back to the present. "No word from their official leaders but the evidence cannot be ignored. We don't know much regarding who these two witches are or why they are trying to drown humans—"

"That's not what happened. They were trying to kill us." Leah kept shaking her head, her hands in her lap.

On the screen, Roland used his magic to create a wave that smashed the humans into the rocks. Careful editing had made it look like Roland was the one starting the encounter, rather than the other way around. The screen changed to show Leah on the ground, her hand out as she used magic, as well. Though he couldn't tell exactly what kind of spell she was doing, the effect of the editing was the same. It looked as if she and Roland were causing harm to humans with no cause.

It wasn't good. Wasn't good at all.

Ryder threw caution to the wind and put his arm around Leah's shoulders. She immediately sank into his hold. "We know that. The media twists what it doesn't understand. And sometimes it deliberately twists what it does."

The anchor continued her news story. "We also have

unconfirmed reports that the witches are in talks with the wolves. As you know, the wolves were forced to come out into the public eye in a shocking way. Since then, there have been numerous reports of violence on both sides. The public is scared, and Washington has issued statements, but no action has been taken on the wolf problem. No word yet how the witch problem will factor into this matter."

Gideon growled loudly, then turned off the screen as the news switched to the weather broadcast.

"What have we done?" Leah whispered, her gaze on her clasped hands. "The Coven will want my head for this." She murmured something so low that even his wolf ears didn't catch it. He'd have asked her what she said, but he wanted to wait until they were alone.

And because he'd been an idiot and said she could stay with him, they would be alone. Often. He, apparently, had a need for pain and tension, because having her stay with him and his wolf without being able to do anything about it would be akin to torture.

"We'll figure it out," Brie said softly from the other sofa. She sat next to her mate with Walker on her other side. Both men had subtle looks of doubt on their faces, and Ryder hoped Leah couldn't read that.

Gideon ran a hand over his face. "We need to meet with the Coven."

Brandon cleared his throat, a frown on his face. "We have a meeting in four days. It's our first one with the Redwood and Talon group."

"I should be there," Gideon added.

Ryder shook his head. "No, you shouldn't. Remember, they're the ones that summoned you. We can't let you show up as Alpha and make them think that is an acceptable way to act toward wolves. While we're on the verge of war and change with the humans, we can't forget that we're in a political dance with the Coven, as well."

Gideon let out a breath. "I hate that. But that's why we have an Heir," he said with a snort. "You'll be my voice?"

Ryder met his brother's, his Alpha's, gaze. "Always." Always the Alpha's voice. Never his own. That was his duty as Heir.

You're nothing. You'll fuck it up like everything. The witches will war. The humans will revolt. You'll drown in the blood of your people like the bastard pup you are.

Again, he ignored the voice. He had to if he wanted to survive.

But do you want to survive? Wouldn't it be easier if you let it all go? They don't need you. They never did.

Leah put her hand on his knee and he looked down into her dark blue eyes. "Ryder?"

He took a deep breath and tried to look normal. It was how he'd made it this long. It was how he would now.

"We'll meet with the Coven and try to come up with a plan," Ryder said finally. "The witches are in the public eye now, and as you can see, they're lumping them together with us. We don't know what Washington's plan is, but we heard what the Senator said in his broadcast, remember? He told the humans to stand together on the other side of the invisible line we hadn't wanted to form. He made it us against them. We need to keep informed. None of us want bloodshed, and to try and prevent that, we'll need to ensure that we're communicating with the others."

Gideon nodded and ran a hand through his beard before tangling his fingers with Brie's. "Parker is out with the other Packs around the country. We're staying in communication with them, but it's hard to keep everyone's priorities in line with so much history."

Parker was a Redwood wolf who had been born a Talon wolf and was now on a journey to each Pack around the country. It might have been easier to meet along digital lines with each Alpha, but centuries of tradition had to be accounted for. The Brentwoods themselves were each over a century old and had a certain way of doing things. He and his family may have acclimated to the changing of the times far easier than most, but not all wolves had. Eventually, each Alpha would have to meet to come up with a joint plan, as every wolf was part of this, not just the Talons and Redwoods. Though because of where the Unveiling had occurred, it was the Talons and Redwoods that were in the public eye. The other Packs were still in hiding, for now, but Ryder knew that wouldn't be for long. There was only so much magic and warding available before those looking for the supernatural in earnest found it.

"We're not going to figure it all out sitting in Walker's living room," Brie said softly. "It's not as easy as making a plan on our own and trying to stick to it. We don't know what the humans have planned, and we don't know what the witches truly want." She met Leah's gaze. "We'll try to find out, though. You said you weren't theirs; so you can be ours for as long as you need to be."

Ryder swallowed hard at Brie's open nature. If Leah were to remain, it would make it that much harder to push her away. He couldn't mate her, no matter what fate said. And he knew the only way to ensure Leah was safe was for him to tell her everything. Perhaps not everything, but enough so she knew there would be no future between them.

It was the only way.

Even if it hurt.

And again, he needed to get his head out of his ass and stop worrying about his own problems. There were wars, meetings, plans, people's lives, and other worries to focus on. Not his own doomed future.

"I...thank you," Leah whispered. "I'm not usually this... frazzled? I guess that's the word for it."

"You were just shot and have been through a horrible ordeal," Brie said softly. "You're allowed to be frazzled."

Ryder's wolf scraped at him again, and this time, he knew he'd pushed the wolf too far. He'd have to get through the next steps with Leah, and then he'd go on a run. He needed to let his wolf out, let his wolf breathe. He might have control, but it was on a weathered leash.

"I think it's time I show Leah where she'll be staying for as long as she needs," Ryder blurted. "It's been a long day."

Brie nodded at him with understanding—maybe a little too much understanding. As much as Ryder loved the fact that his family was close, sometimes, they saw more than he wanted them to. Add in the fact that they were wolves and there was no hiding scents and muttered curses... Ryder knew it was time to go.

"We'll see you soon," Brie said. "Do you need anything to eat? We can send something over."

Ryder shook his head as he stood, bringing Leah with him. "I have provisions, but thank you, little sister." He winked at her, though he didn't feel as jovial as he tried to appear. His head hurt, his heart hurt, and frankly, his soul hurt. And he hadn't done anything to warrant it. Yet.

He nodded at his brothers as Leah tucked her hand into his. He didn't freeze, but it was close. They'd sat together, he'd held her to his side, and yet, with her tiny hand in his, his heart stopped. Just a simple touch, one that would mean nothing to some, made his wolf hope for more. But he knew it wouldn't happen. Again, enough with that.

As he turned with his hand over Leah's, Brandon took a step forward. The warmth of Brandon's powers, so inherent to his brother that Ryder knew sometimes Brandon couldn't control it—even if he wanted to—brushed his skin.

Brandon could take in deep emotions, wash away part of the sadness, help the happiness grow, or entrench himself in one's agony so the sufferer wasn't alone. Yet, each time, it came with a price.

A price Ryder wasn't willing to pay. Nor would he let Brandon pay it, as his little brother always had in the past. Holding the weight of the emotions of a Pack in turmoil was more than one wolf could take. Yet Brandon was forced to do it. Just as Ryder was forced to speak for his Alpha, his Pack, and never for himself.

Leah wasn't Pack, so she wouldn't feel what Brandon was trying to do, but Ryder did.

"Stop."

One word, and Brandon's face went blank. Ryder didn't know what it meant, but he didn't have the energy to deal. Instead, he squeezed Leah's hand and led her outside and in the direction of his place. He picked up her small bag on the way, knowing it was most likely all she had in the world. While he knew his life wasn't perfect, at least he had his family and Pack to lean on in times of sorrow.

Leah had no one.

No one but him.

And yet he couldn't give her what she needed.

"I can't believe the world knows," Leah said softly as they walked through the den toward his place. He wasn't far from Walker's so they didn't need to drive, but it was long enough that the cooling weather relieved his too-warm skin.

"It came as a bit of a shock when we were outed, as well," Ryder replied. "Though I don't know how much longer we could have realistically stayed hidden."

"I know. Everyone is watched. The world is under a digital microscope, and yet the moon goddess protected all of us for centuries. It seems feeble that people with a different agenda were the ones to reveal us."

He squeezed her hand again; aware that the Packmates who watched them walk past were curious. Ryder didn't normally walk with a woman down the center of the den. He wasn't a monk, but it had been a while since he'd paid any attention to a member of the opposite sex. Not only did he have to be careful because of his rank in the Pack and the fact that he'd never wanted his wolf to find his mate, but he also had the voices to battle.

Things weren't always as clear as some would like.

His wolf howled at him, wanting to claim Leah and call it a day. Ryder wanted to simultaneously run away and bring her into his arms. If things were going to work out, if he were going to help her survive and figure out the witch problem, he needed to lay out the issues. He needed to tell her what his wolf wanted, and at least part of why they couldn't be together.

Hell.

He opened his front door and let her enter first. As he closed the door behind him, he ignored the curious glances aimed his way from the people outside. He'd deal with those later.

They made their way into the kitchen, and he pulled out a couple of glasses for water. He'd need to feed them eventually, and probably show her around, but first, he needed to figure out what to do with his hands.

"I don't know how I ended up here." Leah let out a frustrated breath. "I feel like I'm walking through a fog and I can't find my way out. One minute, I'm running for my life; the next, I'm somehow living with a man I don't know." She met Ryder's gaze. "Why am I here, Ryder? Why do I feel this pull to you? Is it magic? Because it's not my magic."

Ryder ran a hand through his hair. There was only one way to do this. Either way, it would hurt, but putting it out there clear and concise would make it easier. At least, he hoped.

"We're mates."

Her eyes widened fractionally. "I had guessed that." She tilted her head, looking so much like a wolf it surprised him. "And yet, you don't sound happy about it."

She'd guessed? Well, he supposed that made sense. Witches grew up learning the stories of mates and wolves.

"The moon goddess blessed wolves with the ability to form a mating bond. With that bond comes an understanding of true harmony. Your soul will literally be touching another through that bond. Sometimes, the mating urge comes as quick as an intake of breath and it's mating at first sight. Sometimes, it takes years for the wolf to trust enough to sense an ability to mate. Through a mating bond comes connection...but not love. That comes from the human half."

She shook her head then leaned against the counter. "So you're saying your wolf wants me." She met his gaze. "But the human half doesn't."

His chest ached, but he didn't nod, nor did he shake his head. "I didn't say that."

"No, but you're not truly explaining yourself either. I don't know you, Ryder. And you don't know me. It's okay that you don't love me. I mean, I think this is our first true conversation without anyone around. It's not like we're in a fairy tale with hearts and stars in our eyes. I don't love you. I don't even know you."

He didn't know why that annoyed him, but he wasn't going to think about it. He needed to get his point across and finish his explanation.

"In a wolf's long lifetime, they can find more than one potential mate. But never once the bond is in place. So, if for some reason, the first person they find doesn't work out or they find themselves friends rather than mates, they can find true mates later. Or, if the worst happens and a mate dies, they can mate again." He thought of the darkness in another's eyes, thought of the secrets that person held, but pushed that away. Those secrets would be revealed later. They had to, or that person would fade away into an eternity of pain.

Again, he needed to move past the thoughts in his head and work on the words that wouldn't seem to come.

"Do you have another mate in mind?" she asked, her voice emotionless.

He cursed. "No. I don't have any mate in mind. That's the point."

Her eyes widened again. "So, that means what?"

He took a step forward and put his hand out, only to let it fall. "My wolf wants you, but the man can't have you." Won't. "So, even though the mating urge will ride hard, know you're safe from me. There will be nothing between us but friendship. If that's what you want. Or, if you'd prefer nothing, then you can stay with one of my siblings. They will keep you safe while you heal and decide what your plan is."

She studied his face, and he'd have given the world to have the power to hear her thoughts. His wolf raged inside, screaming at him to take the words back. His wolf didn't understand. He never did. He didn't know why the flipside of Ryder's powers was so horrible. He only saw the woman in front of them, the one woman for them. The wolf only saw rejection from the human it was supposed to trust with everything it had, not the full extent of the agony Ryder felt.

And yet, Ryder felt what the wolf did, so all in all, his

world was ending deep inside the cavernous depths of his soul. But he had to remain stoic.

He couldn't tell her that he was saving her from a life of anguish and a grey existence. He couldn't tell her because he'd never told a soul why he was the quiet one. He'd never told his family why he was the one to curl into himself when he should have been the one to stand proudly beside his Alpha.

"I can't think about this, Ryder. It's too much. I know you had to get it off your chest, but that's all it can be right now."

She raised her chin.

"You may not want to tell me why you feel that you can't have a mate right now. Maybe someday you will. And maybe one day when I'm not grieving and freaking the fuck out over my life, I'll listen. But for now, I just want to go to bed. Can I do that? Can I just sleep? Maybe I'll wake up and it'll all be a dream."

"We can do that," he said after a tense moment. "I didn't mean to make your burden worse than it already is."

She shook her head and held up her hand. "I get it. If you hadn't explained, I'd honestly just be thinking about what the magic within me wants. I'm going to stay here, though, rather than go somewhere else. I might not know what to do with the magic that flows through my veins every day, but I trust the way it helps me know what choices to make. So I want to stay here. I feel safe with you. Even if I don't understand why."

His wolf scraped the inside of his skin, this time leaving jagged marks along his body. He needed to shift. Now. Yet the fact that she trusted him calmed him enough to know he'd be able to make it to the edge of the woods rather than shift in front of her.

"I'll show you to your room," he said woodenly.

She followed him to the back of the house and stayed silent as he showed her around the guest room and bathroom. There was a stack of clothes on the bed that smelled of Brynn, and he couldn't help but think that his sister saw far too much. All the Brentwoods did.

He let out a shaky breath as his claws slid through the skin on his fingertips.

Time was up.

"I need to go on a run," he growled out.

She turned on her heel and stared at him. Whatever she saw didn't scare her openly, but he knew if he didn't get out of there fast, he couldn't be responsible for his actions.

"Go," she said simply.

"I'll turn on the security panel for you. When I get back, I'll get your handscan tuned in so you can come and go as you please." Sweat beaded on his brow and he dug his claws into his skin, the slight sting of pain relieving his wolf ever so slightly.

He nodded at her, refusing to touch her, though his wolf demanded it, and walked as quickly as he could out of his house and toward the woods. He couldn't let the others know how close to the edge he was. He couldn't let them down. If they saw him now, they'd lose their faith in his abilities to protect them. And at a time where they needed all the faith they could get, his breakdown would be disastrous.

When he reached his secret part of the woods where the

trees gathered to form a sort of glen, he fell to his knees. He clawed off his clothes, too far gone to save them. He'd have to go home as wolf, but he couldn't care right then.

He pulled on the thread that connected wolf to man and let the change come. Each wolf changed differently, the pain coming in waves for some, warm agony for others.

For him, it was torture—depravity and chaos each time.

It didn't ease as he aged, didn't lessen with practice.

Instead, he screamed inwardly as bones broke, tendons tore, and his skin flayed itself over and over. His body became sweat-slick, and he emptied his stomach until it became dry heaves. Usually, he shifted enough and controlled his wolf with enough strength that he didn't show the others his pain.

But when he fought his wolf like this he couldn't hold back.

When he was finally wolf, his body ached and his joints felt as if they'd been glued together wrong. He threw back his head and howled, knowing the others would hear his song, but hopefully not register the meaning behind it.

He'd run through the woods, let the wind and magic of his den flow through his fur and allow his wolf to mourn the loss of what they could never have.

Ryder had been born with the secret darkness of a long-lost tradition and had kept it close to his heart all this time. He'd known he'd have to break his soul and wolf when he finally met the one woman who could be his, but he hadn't known it would hurt like this.

He'd lost his future before he'd even had a chance to venture on the path. And yet, it was for the best. It had to be.

Because if it weren't, all of this was for nothing. And with the world's foundation crumbling beneath their feet, he couldn't afford to wallow in the pity of his decisions. He'd have to move on and show the world—and Leah—he was strong.

It was just another lie in a sea of many. But he would do it. For her. For him. For everyone.

STRATEGY

General Keith Montag did not believe in failure. At least not his. For if he failed, then it was because the ones around him hadn't excelled to their true potential. For the most part, he didn't allow others to fail around him. Therefore, he didn't fail.

So when his men had come up empty when it came to their prey, he'd punished them.

They didn't deserve to breathe another breath, but he couldn't have humans dying until the time was right. Of course, a few had died when the male witch fought back, but Montag had used that to his advantage. Leaking the video to the media had been the plan all along, but the fact that his men had died in the process had only made the reveal that much sweeter.

Now the population was not only scared of the raving beasts, but also of the abominations that looked human.

He'd use that fear.

He always did.

Of course, the plan hadn't gone the way he'd truly wanted it to. He'd wanted to take the twin witches in to study them. The matching set of water witches would have helped his research tenfold. The one that had led him on the path to the witches had promised him that their potential was unmatched. Montag had wanted to use that for his men, either by finding a way to harness that power or by having them join him on his side of unity.

Then the witches had fought back in a way he hadn't predicted.

They'd also run to the damn wolves and gotten too close for comfort.

His men had shot the witches, and the wolves had taken the bodies. He still didn't know if they were alive or dead, but what he did know was that he didn't have them in hand. He'd find out what happened and do what he could to get them back. The one that had betrayed the twins in the first place had promised great things, and Montag wanted everything that came with that.

His men had failed.

And that couldn't be allowed.

His men had been unsuccessful at taking care of the wolf problem a year ago on that grassy hill during the Unveiling, as well.

He was becoming impatient. And when he was impatient, people died.

Montag stormed through the building, glancing through the circle windows in each door. Screams echoed from the rooms as the experiments continued, but Montag only thought of that as progress. Without loss, without study, he couldn't move on to the next phase. Wolves and witches cried and growled, but their bodies were part of the science that came with his strategy.

The coppery scent of blood in the air just proved that progress was being made.

He passed the chambers where the cages lay and entered the large gym where his men trained. They were his secret team, one that would lead to great things. They didn't know it yet, but these human soldiers would be his greatest accomplishment in the supernatural world.

There were twenty men. The best of the best, hand-picked for this assignment. Only they didn't know the extent of their duties—nor did they know what went on beneath their feet. Soon, Montag would enlighten them. But first, he needed them trained.

His best soldier was a man named Shane Bruins. The man was a machine—smart, agile, and strong as hell. If it weren't for the fact that Bruins seemed to think more than he should, he'd be perfect. The damn man didn't exactly question orders, but Montag could see the thoughts in his eyes.

Bruins would be the first to see the next step of his strategy.

Then Bruins would question no more.

He'd be Montag's perfection.

His plan.

His immortality.

CHAPTER
FIVE

I f Leah were a wolf, she would howl at the moon until the pain within her soul didn't feel so deep. The irony of her situation, her presence within the den, was not lost on her, but it didn't help alleviate the agony.

They were burying her brother today.

Never again would she hear his laugh, see the water dance along his skin as he played a game. She'd never see him smile or see him spell. He would never find a woman to love, who would love him in return. He would never raise little babies and let her hold them. Those babies would never call her Aunt Leah. She would never be able to spoil them and show them water tricks to play on their dad.

All of it lost in a moment of terror and panic.

And yet, it didn't seem quite real.

Because they weren't part of a coven, Roland wouldn't be put to ground like their ancestors. Of course, their mother hadn't been either, as she'd died in a hovel, out of sight of those who would shame her and her children. As each year passed, Leah knew her fate would be the same.

She would die alone and be buried within land that was not hers.

However, the wolves buried her brother with the same care they would have their Pack. They bowed their heads and said their prayers to the goddess. Gideon and Brandon spoke words of solace while the neighboring Pack, the Redwoods, sent some of their own to honor Roland.

She didn't understand the depth of their devotion to peace and the strength of the Pack, but she knew she would be forever grateful for these moments.

As she would be forever grateful to Ryder, who stood by her side the entire time. He never spoke a word, but held her hand and let her cry when she needed to. He didn't bring her close or whisper platitudes. No words would help at the moment, and Ryder seemed to understand that.

When they let the final pieces of earth fall between their fingers over Roland's grave, Leah shut off a part of herself. She couldn't function while grieving, and she needed every ounce of her strength to survive. She was living among the wolves for the time being, but that could turn on a dime. She didn't know who was after her in truth, but now she needed to figure it out because the world knew witches were real. Not only that, but she also had a feeling the Coven wasn't too happy with her.

Of course, they had never been happy with her.

Hence why she'd lived the way she had for so long.

"Are you ready to go?" Ryder asked, his voice low.

The Brentwoods had each come to her to give their

condolences, but the other Pack members had kept their distance. It made sense, as they didn't know her but had still come to pay their respects. Either that or they had come to see the witch who had broken the news to the world.

She looked over her shoulder at the burial plot that would one day be covered in flowers and nodded. "Yes. I'm ready."

"Leah?"

She turned at the soft voice behind her.

A strikingly beautiful woman with raven-black hair and light brown skin stood next to a tall, very muscular, and very sexy black man. He stood straight but almost hovered over her without actually hovering. It was as if he had to be near her but couldn't be close at the same time.

She had no idea how she truly knew that, other than the fact that she was a water witch, and sometimes her empathy clung to those around her that her magic needed to touch. She'd never had the chance to practice, as she hadn't stayed in one place long enough to form the connections needed. The magic had never worked with her mother or twin— probably because they were her blood and had similar gifts. The fact that she could feel it so quickly with some of the Talons—and now some of the Redwoods from the look of it —surprised her.

"Charlotte, Bram." Ryder's voice startled her, but she did her best not to show it. "Leah, these are my friends from the Redwood Pack. Charlotte is Maddox and Ellie's daughter, who you met earlier. Bram is a soldier."

If she remembered correctly, soldiers were wolves in the center of the dominant hierarchy that could move up to enforcers or lieutenants depending on the Pack. Their strength of wolf and dominance was ever-changing. Leah was pretty sure all wolves were able to move up and down the totem pole other than those who were in the royal line. Those titles were given to them by the goddess and only changed when the next generation grew into power.

It was funny, really. Wolves were the ones portrayed as barbaric while witches were either seen as crones or naked women dancing peacefully under the moonlight. And yet, it was her people who killed and tortured for their place in the Coven. Wolves let their goddess decide and used their claws and teeth to define their true place, but never to take over a Pack.

She nodded and shook their hands, trying not to let her magic pour out of her and wrap around the couple who seemed to not quite be a true couple. Sometimes she hated her powers and her lack of control.

"Hello," she finally said, aware that her thoughts kept pulling her out of the present.

"I'm so sorry about your brother," Charlotte said softly. "I know you don't know me, but if you need to talk, I'm a good listener."

Leah studied the other woman and felt a connection she couldn't understand. It was as if her inner powers knew Charlotte had been through her own form of torture and pain. Indeed, it seemed this woman would understand her.

"Thank you."

Bram gave her a solemn nod and followed Charlotte as she turned away, leaving Ryder and Leah alone.

"What is their story?" she asked. She hadn't meant to say

anything, as it wasn't her business, but, apparently, she couldn't help it.

"I don't know," Ryder said. "I tend to keep out of matings."

"They're mates?" she asked as she turned to him. He hadn't shaved so his beard was just a bit longer than it had been a couple of days ago. She wanted to run her hands over it, but she couldn't. She wouldn't.

"I don't know. They don't have the bond, but there's something between them anyway." He shrugged. "They're Redwoods, not Talons, so my wolf can't tell much for sure. I can only assume from body language alone at this point."

"I see." She looked over her shoulder at her brother's grave and frowned. "I think it's time to go. If I stay here, I won't leave at all."

Ryder took her hand and led her away. She let out a sigh, but followed him, knowing she was leaving her past behind with each step and stepping into a future she couldn't quite understand.

When they made it back to Ryder's, she went back to her room and stripped off her clothes. She didn't want to wear the black anymore. She'd have burned them or thrown them away, but they were borrowed from the Pack. Instead, she changed into a pair of leggings and a long-sleeved tunic. Ryder had been silent on the walk back, but she knew it wasn't her. He never spoke unless it was important, and she kind of liked that. The silence wasn't awkward, but comforting.

She met her gaze in the mirror and knew it was time to tell him everything. She was a guest within the Talon walls and couldn't hide from the world. Her problems would find her...and soon.

When she made her way out to the living room. Ryder was on the couch, looking at his tablet. She knew all the Talons had jobs of their own, or at least they used to before the Unveiling. She wasn't sure what Ryder's was or if he still had it. But asking him now would only delay what she needed to say. If they let her remain within the wards, she'd ask him, though. He might not want her as his mate, but she still felt a strong enough connection that she wanted to know who he was.

"Ryder?"

He looked up from his tablet, his blue eyes intense. He must have heard her shuffle in, but he'd let her breathe first. "What is it, Leah?"

"I want to tell you why I was running."

He nodded but didn't stand up, didn't gesture for her to sit next to him. He was letting her make the choice. Goddess, she could fall for him. But she wouldn't. She had to protect the one thing she had left—her heart.

"Okay."

"I used to belong to the Coven. The one you are meeting soon."

His eyebrows rose, but he didn't say anything.

"Well, I suppose you could say I belonged until I was born. My mother, you see, was shunned when she became pregnant with Roland and me."

Ryder's nostrils flared, but again, he didn't say anything.

"She had been having an affair with a witch who was already married. Of course, she hadn't known that until it was too late. Witches do not live in dens, nor do they know all of each other as well as wolves seem to. She didn't know this witch was on his way to becoming the leader of the Coven by using any means necessary. She didn't know his wife was just as brutal with the ice in her veins as her husband was with his ability to drown others with just a thought. When my mother became pregnant, she was shunned, as I said. But that wasn't all. The man who is my father by biology and nothing more did not have children with his wife. She couldn't, you see. But that didn't mean he wanted bastards running around with his blood in their veins. He was always afraid of what powers we could have. He is powerful. Oh so powerful. And he was afraid any child from his loins would be so formidable they'd overthrow him." She paused. Took a breath. "I don't know what decree he made exactly, but the result was my mother's death. The humans may have killed my brother, but I wouldn't put it past my father to have been the one to lead the way. I've been running all my life, Ryder. I'm tired. And yet, the world now knows witches are real and the Coven will want my head for more than one reason. I will have to face the Coven, Ryder. I will have to face my fate."

Ryder stood up then. He took the four steps that separated them and stood right in front of her. When he cupped her face, she stopped breathing, rendered unable to think by his touch.

"They will not have you, Leah. One day I will tell you the story of the Alpha and Heir of the Pack before Gideon and me. I will tell you how they did the same thing to another woman as the Coven did to your mother. I was too young, too weak to protect that woman and her child, but I know them now. Know they are safe as Redwoods where they weren't as Talons. We will not allow you...I will not allow you to be given up to the Coven like a sacrifice. We will work it out. I am meeting with the Coven in two days, and you will come with me. We will face this head-on."

She sucked in a breath, her lungs burning. "Ryder..."

"They will not have you. Your father, if you can call him that, was the one in the wrong. He had no right to call upon your death, no matter what Coven decree he made. I don't care what they think. As for what happened on camera? I was part of the Unveiling. I was one of the wolves who were shown to the world. And yet, I live. I will not allow you to be punished for others' actions."

"You can't tell the Coven what to do, Ryder. It's not that easy."

"Then we'll make it that easy." His thumb brushed her cheek, sending shivers down her spine. "You deserve more than a life on the run, more than a Coven to punish you." His voice lowered. "You deserve more than me."

With that, he brushed his lips over hers, once, twice, in the gentlest of kisses. She closed her eyes, relishing the slight pressure of his lips to hers.

It was over before it had begun, but she knew that kiss had meant something.

Only it didn't mean everything.

Because despite the fact that he'd kissed her; despite the fact that he'd promised he would protect her; she would have to protect herself. She wasn't good enough for him, wasn't his mate in truth.

She was just a witch with no home.

Forever alone.

––––––––

RYDER CLOSED his eyes and told himself he was ready for what was to come. It was only a meeting between two Packs and a Coven of witches that would set the tone for their relationship during a time of war and uncertainty.

Add in the fact that his wolf craved the woman at his side and that the woman came from a dark past of betrayal and abandonment tied to that exact Coven, and Ryder knew there were more questions than answers.

No pressure at all.

"I'm not trying to read your emotions, but you're screaming them at me," Brandon said from his side.

Ryder had heard his brother come to his side, of course, but he hadn't said anything. There wasn't much to say with everything going on in his mind. He didn't particularly like Brandon's powers as Omega. He wanted his emotions to remain his own, but he knew Brandon couldn't control it.

"Unless I'm about to break down and tear off the Coven leader's head, just ignore them."

Brandon let out a sigh. "I can't ignore it," he said softly, almost a whisper. "I never can. Speaking of Coven leaders, are you going to be able to handle Leah at your side while you meet her father?"

Leah had told his family about her connections to the Coven the day before so there wouldn't be any surprises. His siblings had taken it surprisingly well. Leah would be joining them for the meeting, not as a representative for the Talons, but as a guest who needed to be present because of what had brought her to their den in the first place.

Ryder hadn't said Leah was his mate or that he'd rejected the mating urge and bond.

He should have known he wouldn't be able to hide it from Brandon.

"I won't hurt the Pack," he growled out.

"Never thought you would. I'm more worried about you hurting yourself."

Ryder turned to his brother. "Leave it, Brandon."

Brandon just met his gaze, not quite a challenge, but close enough. Ryder was Heir, slightly higher in rank than the Omega. Their dominance couldn't be changed, but they could piss off their wolves.

"What's going on?" Leah asked as she came up to them. She'd gone to a nearby stream as soon as they'd made it to the meeting location so she could wash her hands. She'd been nervous and had needed the water for her magic. Ryder had been able to hear her the entire time, and would have run to her side in a moment if there were trouble. And since they were on neutral ground and not within wards, trouble could come at any moment.

Because they were in the middle of a forest, they had some cover in case there was an issue, at least. With the humans always on the hunt, and hate groups hidden around the area, Ryder wasn't going to take chances. As soon as the Redwood Heir and Omega arrived, they'd make their way into the meeting area and get started. He didn't like being out in the open as they were.

"Ryder?"

He shook his head at Leah's words. "Nothing's going on. We're just having a brother issue."

She studied his face then licked her lips. He wanted to do the same but held himself back.

The sound of two people coming through the trees, purposely stepping hard as to announce their presence, hit his ears and he turned on his heel, grabbing Leah's wrist and tugging her close at the same time.

She didn't pull away, but he did feel water sliding up his fingers. It seemed his little witch was more powerful than he thought.

No, not his witch.

He needed to remember that.

As soon as he inhaled and scented Finn and Drake, the Heir and Omega of the Redwood Pack, he relaxed marginally. He couldn't relax fully, as he had Leah at his side and his wolf craved her more than air, but at least he didn't feel as if he were in more danger than usual.

"You ready?" Finn asked, his wolf in his eyes. His new brother-in-law was one damn strong wolf and had recently increased his strength after almost dying for his bond with Brynn. It was good to have him on their side rather than the enemy's.

Everyone nodded before taking deep breaths and starting their way to the official meeting place. Instead of meeting on anyone's land, they were going to meet in an older building that was not claimed by either wolf or witch.

As soon as they entered the building, Ryder's senses went on alert. There hadn't been a sentry on duty, but there had been magic. He'd felt it on his skin, and Leah had let out a slight gasp. His wolf pushed against him, but she didn't scent of pain, only surprise, so he didn't mention it. He couldn't let others know there might be a weakness.

"You've made it, wolf," a deep voice with a slightly nasal tone said.

Leah's hand brushed his arm discreetly, and he wanted to pull her behind him to shield her. Only to do so would undermine her own strength.

Ryder raised his chin and met the gaze of an older man with dark hair, sprinkled with white and grey. His pointed nose and chin made him look aristocratic, but he had Leah's blue eyes.

This was the Coven leader.

Leah's father.

The man who'd abandoned her, shunned her, and called for her death.

Ryder's wolf growled, pushed, and scraped. Yet on the outside, he looked cool, calm, and collected. That was one of his strengths. It had kept him alive through the worst.

While his gaze was on the man in front of him, his senses were on the others around him. Six witches sat around the leader, men and woman in dark robes with frowns on their faces.

But they weren't alone.

Dozens of spirits lined the walls. He'd never seen so many at once. His skin grew cold and his lungs seized. He couldn't allow the others to see his reaction, couldn't let them know what he saw. The spirits looked at him, frowns on their faces, as well. Some screamed. Others called his name, called for his death, for his life. They didn't move forward, and he wasn't sure if they could.

It seemed to him that these spirits were of the Coven, ancestors of the seven breathing witches that stood in front of him.

Interesting.

And scary as hell.

He'd been born with the power to hear and see the dead, been born with another, darker power, as well. And yet he didn't know what to do with it.

However, this wasn't the time. He met the leader's eyes and set his jaw. The other man finally lowered his gaze, and Ryder's wolf was satisfied. He might not be the Alpha, but he was damn strong, and this fucking peon in front of him couldn't match his strength. He wouldn't ignore the magic within, but he knew Leah was stronger than her father, as well. Knew deep in his bones.

He just didn't think she knew that.

But from the look of pure hatred in the other man's eyes, her father knew it.

"I am Ryder, Heir of the Talon Pack." His voice was strong, not a hint of anger, just pure wolf.

"I am Finn, Heir of the Redwood Pack."

"I am Brandon, Omega of the Talon Pack."

"I am Drake, Omega of the Redwood Pack."

"And I am Leah. Daughter of the moon goddess and water witch."

They hadn't planned what they would say, and yet what they had said sounded as if it were buried deep within tradition and meaning. That Leah would use those exact words made his wolf sing. Damn the Coven for shunning her.

"You dare bring that abomination in our presence!"

"Luis!" One of the younger female witches called.

"Quiet, Diana. You know the law. This witch, Leah, is an abomination and should never have been born."

"An abomination?" Leah asked, her voice deadly quiet. "Or just your bastard?"

The woman by Luis's side hissed. "You are not my husband's child. You are nothing. You should have been killed when you were born."

"My wife, Darynda, is correct. If you hadn't been born, the witches would be safe. Now the world knows we are real. They will burn us at the stake as they did a century ago. You have caused our ruin." Luis stood up and pointed his finger. Water wrapped around his arm in a rush of waves but didn't lash out.

Ryder let out a growl and barely resisted the urge to roll his eyes. So dramatic, these witches.

"We aren't here to have you call for her death. She is ours." Ryder's words surprised even him. Brandon stiffened by his side but relaxed so quickly Ryder wasn't sure anyone else had seen it other than perhaps Finn and Drake.

"Yours? She's a wolf, then? You want to start our negotiations with a threat?"

Ryder smiled, then. It wasn't a happy one, and from the way some of the Coven members paled, he knew his point had gotten across.

"It wasn't a threat. It's a promise. As for our negotiations... You know as well as I do that our meeting today is just that, a meeting. We are not enemies. We never have been. You summoned our Alpha, and he is not here because you do not summon a wolf. We are here because our people are dying. Your people are dying. The humans are running scared right now, but soon they will formulate a plan and we could all be in their hands in the end."

Luis opened his mouth to speak, but Finn cut him off.

"We will meet again to discuss our plans. We want to live in a world where we can be free and not threatened. I can see we've started off on the wrong foot. Because of that, we will be back again at a later time to discuss our options." Finn met Ryder's eyes and nodded. "The humans who came after the Packs and then after Leah are the ones at fault. Not a witch who was trying to protect herself. I see no proof she's an abomination, nor do I know what the hell that even means. So, yeah. She's with us."

"So it's wolves versus witches, then?" Luis snarled.

"It's not anything as of yet," Ryder answered. "We will begin again, but know this, we are wolves, we are strong. We have fought by your side before, have always worked with you to protect our secrets, but we are Pack. Never forget that."

On that note, he turned on his heel and the others followed. The witches began to fight within their Coven, screaming at one another, but Ryder let that go. He needed to get Leah and Brandon within the ward walls so he could breathe.

"Ryder," Leah whispered once they were out of hearing range. "You shouldn't have done that. You might have started a war over me. I'm not worth that."

Ryder snarled and turned to her. The others stood around them, not bothering to walk away to give them privacy.

"You are worth that and more," he said and wanted to curse. He hadn't meant to say that. "We do not allow the innocent to get hurt by those in power. And frankly, we wouldn't have given you away to them because we don't do what we're ordered to. They are not my Alpha. And they should know that."

"Ryder..."

Finn let out a breath, then shook his head, a small smile on his face. "Well, that went well."

Ryder snorted. "Fucked up for sure."

Brandon and Drake both rolled their eyes.

"We'll figure it out," Finn said then brought Leah into a hug. It was only because he was mated that Ryder didn't rip Finn's arms off for doing that.

"It was never going to end well," Brandon said. "We were pissed going in because of the summoning. The witches are running scared because of their own Unveiling. But it's not your fault, Leah."

She scowled. "It sure feels like it. I'm not going to allow that to be for nothing, though. I'll help you protect your Pack. I have some power, enough that my father wanted me dead from birth. So I'll do what I can to help you, even as I try to figure out what I'm doing."

Ryder's wolf let out a happy howl, but he didn't let his face say anything. He'd claimed her in front of the Redwoods, his brother, and the witches, and she hadn't said anything about it. He was giving her mixed signals, and yet, he didn't care. He couldn't think when there was so much going on, so much that could go wrong.

The first witch and wolf meeting had gone to hell, but they would figure it out.

There wasn't another choice.

And it didn't take seeing the dead for him to know that with one wrong move, all would be lost.

CHAPTER
SIX

"Is he staring?" Leah asked.

Charlotte's eyes danced and she looked over Leah's shoulder. "No, but he was earlier."

So Ryder wasn't looking at her, but he had been. That sounded about right. He kept changing his damn mind. First he'd pushed her away before he kissed her. Then he'd said he wouldn't mate her, but damn well claimed her in the Coven meeting. She still wasn't sure what that had meant or exactly what the others had thought, but it had meant something. She wasn't Pack, but he'd still said she was his. Or, at least, theirs. It wasn't as if she wanted to marry him and have his babies, but it would be nice if he would make his choice and stick to it.

She'd told herself years ago she wouldn't have children and wouldn't find a man to live her life with. She'd always thought her twin would be able to do that despite the danger, but that wasn't for her. She hadn't wanted her bloodline to continue with her, not with all the pain she'd lived with for so long.

But letting her hands run along that wolf's body as they both panted with need wouldn't be such a bad thing.

Her cheeks heated, and Charlotte raised a brow at her.

"Interesting place your thoughts went, I would think." She smiled and her whole face brightened. The woman was absolutely beautiful, though there was a sadness in her eyes that she couldn't quite hide. Leah knew what Bram saw in the woman, though he, like Ryder, did his best not to stare for too long.

If Leah had planned to stay within the den for any amount of time, she might have asked Charlotte what the story was behind that, but she couldn't. She didn't know her future and what path she would take. Therefore, making friends and promises wasn't for her. It hadn't been the case for more years than she cared to count.

"Leah? Are you okay?"

Charlotte's voice brought her out of her thoughts and she nodded. "Sorry, just woolgathering."

The other woman's head tilted. "Are you sure that's it? You can talk to me, you know. I'm not an Omega or anything close to that, but I'm a good listener." Her words echoed what she'd said at Roland's gravesite, and Leah couldn't take anything away from them but pure honesty.

"I..." She trailed off then tried to look casual as she glanced over her shoulder at Bram, Ryder, and Brandon.

Brandon had come over to Ryder's that morning with coffee and pastries and, apparently, an agenda. The quiet Omega and his Heir brother had been in deep talks since they'd politely asked to speak privately. She didn't feel slighted in the least, as she was the one intruding. She didn't belong with the Talons, didn't belong with anyone, and she knew that. Having two very handsome wolves ask for some space to work without her around wasn't an insult. It was just life.

When Bram and Charlotte had shown up, it had been a surprise. Though not an unwelcome one, as Ryder had opened his home to the two. Bram had quickly joined in whatever conversation the other two men were having, and Charlotte had taken Leah aside to the living room, where they were now.

Any other time, Leah might have felt overwhelmed at the drastic changes in her life and the fact that she was now living with a wolf who wanted her, yet didn't want to want her, as well as being surrounded by wolves who could kill her in an instant. They were that strong. It was only the pureness of their hearts and the integrity of their souls that led them down the path of humanity and away from depravity.

She wasn't a pacifist, but she also preferred to use her words to fight rather than her magic. It just wasn't in her as a water witch. Oh, she would try, and could even inflict some damage if she had to, but she tried not to.

And that wasn't the way to survive on the run.

It had been Roland that saved her countless times because he could work past the inherent calmness of his powers. He had been the storm to her quiet lake.

And now he was gone, and she had to provide the waves.

Leah let out a breath, reaching out to grip Charlotte's hand. The other woman had quietly waited while Leah tumbled through her thoughts.

"One day, I will be able to have a full conversation without getting lost within myself," Leah said simply.

Charlotte just smiled softly and shook her head. "You've been through a lot. I'm surprised you're even out here and not wrapped in your quilt on your bed. Or perhaps in a bath?"

Leah smiled then. "I do love baths." And Ryder had a beautiful claw foot tub in the master bathroom he had offered to her. She hadn't taken him up on the offer yet, as she hadn't wanted to take four hours in the bath when he might need something, but she would soon. Her powers demanded it.

"You know, there's a lake on Talon land, I believe," Charlotte added. She looked over Leah's shoulder. "Ryder, is the lake within the den wards?"

The conversation at the dining room table stopped, and Leah turned as all three men looked over at them. Was it wrong that she heated up just at the thought of Ryder looking at her like that? Sure, the other two were attractive, but, apparently, all she wanted was Ryder.

Who wouldn't take her for a mate.

But she didn't want that, she reminded herself.

Ryder met Leah's gaze and nodded. "It's within the den wards." He kept looking at her, though it had been Charlotte who'd posed the question. "I should have thought of that before. Do you need to recharge? I can take you to the lake tonight."

"I'm fine for now," she said honestly. She hadn't used her powers, and since she'd been able to drink as much water as she wanted plus take long showers, she was fine. A natural lake would be amazing, but it wasn't necessarily needed yet. "I don't want to take you away from your duties or burden you." She didn't want to be anyone's burden, least of all Ryder's.

"You just tell me, and we will go." He paused. "Or someone else can take you, of course. It doesn't have to be me."

So polite. So formal.

She honestly did not understand this wolf.

Nor did she understand herself recently.

"Thanks."

"Let's go for a walk," Charlotte said suddenly. She stood and brought Leah with her. "We'll let you guys talk Pack business or whatever is so interesting over there, and I'll show Leah around."

Ryder snorted. "You're not a Talon, Charlotte. How are you going to show her around?"

Charlotte rolled her eyes. "Between Finn, Gina, and Brie, my family is slowly mating with all of you so much that I'm here just as much as I'm on Redwood land. If I get lost, I'll call Brie." She paused. "Unless you don't want a Redwood and a lone witch walking around without supervision."

Brandon sighed. "It's not that."

"Then what is it?" Leah asked. "Am I a prisoner here?" She couldn't keep the bite out of her tone, and when Brandon sat back, she regretted it. He may not be able to feel her emotions because she wasn't Pack, but he could feel Ryder's.

She kept messing up, and yet because she didn't know where she stood, she couldn't find her balance. That needed to change. She wasn't some weak-kneed girl who couldn't breathe without fainting. And despite how she'd acted since she'd first come to the Talons over a week ago, she needed to show them who she was.

Ryder stood and made his way to her, a frown on his face. Leah took a deep breath, her heart racing, though she wasn't sure why. He didn't move to touch her, didn't do anything but stand closer to her than was necessary for a mere acquaintance.

"You aren't a prisoner. You were always able to leave when you wanted. However, you stayed. You stayed to grieve and to find your next step. Then, two days ago, you told us you would fight alongside us. Or at least stay by our sides as we protect our people. You might not have the bonds to become Pack, but that doesn't mean you're an outsider."

She sighed. "There's a reason I don't have the bonds." She hadn't meant to say that.

He closed his eyes and his nostrils flared. "Leah."

She held up her hands. "I didn't mean that. Charlotte's right. I need some air to clear my head. Go back to your conversation. You say I'm not a prisoner, so prove it."

His jaw clenched. "I don't want you hurt." The words were ripped from him.

"Who would hurt me? I'm going to be in the middle of the den with your people. Are you saying your people don't want me here?" She didn't know why that hurt to think about. It wasn't as if anyone had ever wanted her to be with them. She'd only had her mother and twin for so long, she should have been used to the rejections.

He stayed silent for so long, Leah was afraid she'd over-stepped her bounds. But since she didn't know her bounds to begin with, she wasn't sure what to think.

"Just be careful."

With that, he walked away, leaving Leah as confused as ever. Charlotte rolled her shoulders and took her hand, practically dragging her to the front door. When the door closed behind them, Charlotte let out a breath.

"I do not understand males."

Leah snorted at that. "I never could in the past, and now that everything seems to have gone haywire, I definitely don't now."

Charlotte kept her hand in Leah's and started walking down the path toward the center of the den. "I'm going to ask you something and I'm going to be blunt about it."

Leah let out a breath. "How blunt?"

"Is Ryder your mate?"

Leah stopped moving, forcing Charlotte to do the same. They were still pretty secluded thanks to the trees along the path, so no other Pack members were around to hear, but they could walk up on them at any moment. But for some reason, she found herself wanting to tell Charlotte everything.

"I'm a witch. We don't mate the way wolves do."

Charlotte shook her head. "That's a copout."

"Is Bram your mate?" Leah snapped.

Charlotte's chin rose, her eyes going blank. "You're right. That was too personal. Let's continue to walk."

Leah cursed herself. "I'm sorry. I don't know what the hell is going on. Ryder says I could be his mate. A potential, he called it. Yet he says he won't mate me with. Or rather, I think he said he couldn't. I don't know what that means. He pushed me away, but then he kissed me. He kissed me, Charlotte, but he doesn't want to mate with me. And why should I care? I'm a witch. I might be able to form a mating bond thanks to his wolf, but it's not like I'll pine for him. Right? I don't have a wolf that will break without that bond. But why do I want him like I do? Why am I breaking because he says he doesn't want me, even if his wolf does? And why should I care, when the world is going to shit? Roland died, and I'm worried about a man wanting me as his mate. What is wrong with me?"

Tears slid down her cheeks, and she angrily wiped them away. She hated crying, yet it seemed it was all she could do.

Charlotte pressed her lips together then sighed.

"I want to rip that wolf's face off for you."

Leah's eyes widened at the words. She tended to forget that the people around here shared their beings with the souls of wolves and could shift in an instant. Of course, most forgot she held magic within her veins and could control water.

"I don't know why he said the things he said, but...well... I know that mating isn't easy. It's not just a true declaration and happy thoughts. At least not for anyone I've known. It takes work...and a leap of faith that doesn't come easily to most."

Leah didn't say anything. She wasn't sure what else there was to say.

Charlotte winced. "That came out wrong. Damn it. No wonder you're freaking out. Nothing is coming out the way it should. All I'm saying is if he's doing one thing, and saying another, then you need to talk to him. Mating is hard. It's not always perfect right away. Sometimes things change—people change. If Ryder has a reason for not wanting to mate, find out what it is. If you don't want to mate with him at all, then make sure he knows that. I think you two just need to talk." She sighed. "And nothing I just said helped. I mean, hell, you've been through so much and yet it's not over."

Charlotte looked so stressed; Leah could only do one thing. She wrapped her arms around the other woman and hugged her tightly. Charlotte's arms came around her, and Leah could have sworn she could feel the pain of the woman's wolf. Leah wasn't a wolf, so why could she feel that? This wasn't the first time, and it made her wonder. But she didn't want to think too hard as her brain already hurt enough as it was.

"I don't know what I'm doing," Leah said finally.

"I don't think any of us do." Charlotte pulled back. "Let's walk some more, then head back. I'm pretty sure the guys are talking about Pack dynamics, not the Coven, so we can go back and listen."

"If it were about the Coven, I would assume the others would be there."

"Totally. I know our Packs are allies and are inter-mating, but every once in a while it's good to put an emphasis on our own mental health and the way we can keep our alliance intact."

What would it feel like to have not only a family but also a whole other Pack to care for and care for you? She couldn't even comprehend it.

When they made their way back to the house, she felt slightly better from unloading on Charlotte. It wasn't lost on her that the other woman hadn't told her much about herself, but she didn't mind. If Charlotte ever felt like she could, Leah would be there. Sharing was only a small way to be close to someone—something she'd never done before.

Of course, as soon as she stepped inside the house, all her attention went to Ryder. She couldn't stop thinking about the way his eyes went dark when he looked at her. Or the fact that sometimes she could see a slight gold ring around his irises when his wolf came to the surface. He didn't smile when she came in, but he did study her as if he couldn't help but look at her.

Or maybe that was his wolf and the man would pull away once again.

Charlotte cleared her throat from behind her, and Leah moved to the side. "Bram, we need to go."

Bram stood and nodded. "I know. I was going to call you soon if you hadn't shown up when you did." He turned to Ryder and Brandon. "I'll see you guys tomorrow?"

They nodded, and Bram came toward Charlotte.

"What's tomorrow?" Leah asked.

"You'll see," Bram said and smiled, surprising her. He didn't smile often, but damn, he looked damn sexy when he did. If he and Charlotte were truly mates—no matter how they were handling it—Charlotte was one lucky woman.

Leah found herself alone with Brandon and Ryder and felt awkward. She was always awkward around Ryder. She may be living with him, but she didn't spend much time with him. He had things to do with his family, and she'd been healing and grieving.

Now she was as whole as she was going to get and she had to figure out what she was going to do with him. She might not know what she was going to do about the world knowing about witches, but she could at least figure herself out. Or try to.

Her heart ached a bit and she wasn't sure why. It was Brandon who came to her, though, not Ryder. The Omega studied her face and stopped right in front of her. She sucked in a breath as he cupped her cheek with his hand.

"What worries you, Leah? Your heart hurts so much, I can feel it." He tilted his head. "How can I feel it, Leah? You aren't Pack? Yet I know your pain. Why is that?"

She didn't understand it either. Didn't understand how she felt so close to not only the Talons but the Redwoods, as well. How was it that she could feel a connection to people so quickly, and yet never have had that before?

A low growl filled the room, and Brandon's eyes widened ever so slightly.

"Get your hand off of her, brother," Ryder growled from his spot in the dining room.

Leah didn't move, didn't dare to breathe. She'd heard of wolves and their possessiveness, but she hadn't seen it.

Until now.

And that pissed her off. What right did Ryder have to be possessive of her? He may have kissed her—once—but that didn't mean she was his.

She'd survived on her own all this time.

She was no one's but her own.

She pulled away, rather than let Brandon lower his hand. "Perhaps you should leave," she said softly. She didn't want to get in the middle of brothers, but damn it, she needed to set a few things straight.

Brandon looked over his shoulder at his brother. "We'll talk later. But know you're not alone."

"Go." One word. One growl. And yet, Leah couldn't help the shivers that went down her spine.

Damn, she wished she understood what the hell was going on.

Brandon left after giving her a look of...pity? No. Anticipation maybe? Either way, as soon as he closed the door behind him, she was left in a room with Ryder.

The man who didn't want her, yet wanted her.

The man who she wanted, yet didn't want.

Ryder stalked toward her, his gaze on hers and his hands fisted at his sides. He stopped right in front of her as Brandon had, but instead of freezing, her body tilted toward him of its own accord. She wanted to wrap her body around him and never let go. Yet she also wanted to push him away.

"You're messing with me, Ryder. You can't growl at your brother for touching me. You can't think you own me when you told me yourself you wanted nothing to do with me."

"I never said that." He breathed in through his nose, his chest lifting. "I said I can't mate with you. There's a difference. I fucking want you, Leah. I want you beneath me, over me, around me. I want to sink into your heat and fuck you hard against the wall. I want to grip your hips while I pump into you. I want you so fucking much, Leah. And I can't have you the way my wolf wants you."

She blinked. Shocked. "But..."

"I can't mate with you no matter how much I want to."

"You need to explain that, Ryder. It's not fair to either of us if you don't."

His hand shot out and gripped her hair. He tilted her head back, and she licked her lips. "I will tell you. One day. What do you want, Leah? Because I don't know if I'll be able to hold myself back. I want you. Do you want me? Do you want me as we are? Just for now, just until we can breathe? Maybe the constant want, the constant need will be gone by then. Can you handle that?"

She wasn't sure if she truly understood what the answers to any of those questions were, but she knew she wanted him. That had to count for something.

"So, just for now? Just to take off the edge?" Her voice was breathy, needy.

He traced his other hand down her arm and up again before going across her collarbone. "No promises. But I won't hurt you, Leah. We'll take what we need, but not too much."

She wasn't sure if either of them believed that, but she didn't know if she cared. All she wanted was to forget the pain, forget what had led her here, and forget what might be coming. If she could give in, if only for the moment, she might be able to live again.

"Okay," she said. "But I want to go slower than a hard fuck against the wall. I'm not sure if I'm ready for that."

His eyes narrowed at her vulgarity, but she thought he might have liked it. "I can do that, Leah. I can do that."

Then he crushed his mouth to hers, letting his hand skim down her body to grip her ass. She moaned and rocked into him, wanting more, needing more. He nipped at her lips, growling low so the vibrations went straight through her. His tongue slid along hers, then dominated, surprising the hell out of her.

Ryder was the quiet one. The one who held doors open and soothed and calmed.

Yet this Ryder...dear goddess. He rocked her world. And he'd only kissed her.

Could she call this just a kiss? She wrapped her arms around his waist, trying to pull him closer, but couldn't stop moving her hands to get more of him. She might have been the one to say she wanted to go slow, but hell, she wasn't sure if she could hold back.

Ryder pulled away and met her gaze. "We won't go too far, but I need to touch you, Leah. Let me touch you."

Instead of speaking, she took his hand and placed it on her collarbone where he'd had it before.

The gold in his eyes brightened and he licked his lips, placing his other hand on the other side. "I can do that," he said slyly. He traced her skin with his calloused fingers then went lower. When he cupped her breasts, she pressed into him, her nipples hard pebbles against his palms. He squeezed and molded then lowered one of his hands even more, gently going over her belly.

She leaned against the wall, putting her palms flat against the surface to keep herself steady. Her knees were going weak, and she hadn't even come yet.

And Ryder would make her come. She was sure of it.

When his fingers deftly went beneath the waistband of her leggings, she bit into her lip. He leaned forward and kissed her again, just as hard as before. He rocked into her, his hard cock pressing against her stomach.

When his fingertips brushed along her clit, she moaned into his mouth.

"That's it, little witch. You're so wet for me already. Ride my hand, Leah."

She met his gaze and rocked. His fingers slowly teased her before sliding deep inside. She called out, arching her back as he fucked her with his fingers. When his thumb pressed against her clit, she went right over the edge, coming on his hand and almost falling. Ryder wrapped his arm around her waist and held her up, slowly helping her down from her peak as she tried to catch her breath.

When he removed his hand and brought his fingers to his lips, she almost came again. He licked each one, his gaze never leaving hers as he tasted her on his skin.

"Sweet," he whispered gruffly. "So fucking sweet."

She kissed his jaw, then kissed him again, rather than speaking. She wasn't sure what she'd say anyway. She'd lost herself in him, and they both still had their clothes on. If she worked hard enough, she could separate sex and feelings, but she wasn't sure she'd be able to.

The wolf wanted her. And now the man did, as well.

But they wouldn't have her.

And she'd have to be okay with that. Because she couldn't trust that her life would keep him safe as it was. It was good that they'd kept this with no promises. It was safer that way.

Only she wasn't sure there was any form of safety anymore.

She'd probably made the worst mistake ever. Yet with Ryder's arms around her and his lips on hers, she wasn't sure she cared.

And that might cost both of them more than she'd thought possible.

CHARLOTTE

Charlotte closed her eyes and tried not to cry. Again. She hated crying. She'd grown up knowing if she cried, she'd be punished. And when Ellie and Maddox had taken her in, they'd taught her that emotion was to be celebrated, something that one needed to thrive. Yet if she cried anymore about this particular issue, she'd lose herself.

Again.

What was wrong with her?

She should be happy. She should know that she was blessed.

She'd grown up with the Centrals, the daughter of the Alpha who had called for the demon and the sister of the following Alpha who had killed so many of those she loved. She knew she was tainted, knew she was scarred beyond measure, but did her best so others couldn't see that.

Ellie and Maddox had saved her. They had become her parents and raised her, loving her with all of their hearts.

She was a strong wolf, a strong woman, and one that could stand on her own and fight for her Pack.

And yet it was her wolf and her soul that ached.

Bram, the sexy, dark-skinned wolf who sat next to her was her mate. He was the one wolf in all the world that would complete her soul. If the world were perfect, he would take her into his arms and they would mate and make love, completing the mating bond until they both knew their fate was sealed and perfect.

Yet that hadn't happened.

Bram was her mate.

She was his.

They both knew this. It wasn't like Finn and Brynn where there had been something broken with Finn's wolf.

Bram and Charlotte were each missing something.

They'd been friends for years, and then their wolves had fallen for each other. They'd made love and had known they would create a bond and a future.

Only the bond hadn't formed.

They weren't enough for each other.

Her heart ached for the man at her side, the man that should have been everything, yet wasn't.

It was her.

She was the one messing it up.

They were missing something because of her.

She was tainted. She was unworthy.

Bram couldn't have his future because of the blood in her veins.

And that was something she would have to live with. Because one day soon, she would have to fully cut the ties and let him go. He deserved to find a mate that he could form the bond with. Because she wasn't it. She would remain alone, unmated, unwanted. Because that was her reality. Her price to pay for what she had done before the Redwoods took her in.

Bram let out a breath and looked at her, sending her heart racing as well as the tears sliding down her cheeks.

"Don't cry. I can't take it when you cry."

She let the tears fall, knowing these had to be the last. "I'm sorry."

So sorry. For everything.

She'd lost him before she ever had him. And yet she couldn't allow that to be the only thing that mattered. Maybe if she focused on Ryder and Leah's mating, things would be better. She had nothing else to lose. She'd already lost everything.

Bram sighed and turned away, leaving her heart in pieces in the process.

Again.

CHAPTER
SEVEN

Ryder wiped the sweat from his brow and grinned at his brother. Gideon smiled back, only it was more teeth than anything, and Leah knew things were about to get good.

"You two just going to stand around and glare at each other, or are we going to play some ball?" Finn called out from the other side of the field.

Leah leaned against the large rock behind her and let out a small sigh.

"I know, right?" Brie whispered from her side. "It's like porn out there."

"Those are my brothers, you know," Brynn said from Brie's other side.

"And your mate," Brie said. "And most of the Redwoods are related to me, but I can still watch the shirtless Talons, and my very sexy and sweaty Alpha of a mate play." She let out a long sigh and rested her chin on her knee.

Brynn turned to face her mate, Finn, and let out a sigh of her own.

Leah just shook her head, holding back a smile as the two very happily mated women stared at their mates. Of course, Leah couldn't blame them.

Dear goddess, this had to be the best thing she'd ever seen in her life.

A shifter game of touch football. Shirtless men running into each other, pinning one another down, and bending over as they tried to get to the end zone. Sports porn. Since it was mid-winter, the snow on the ground only heightened the effect of the very sexy, shirtless men. Sweat glistened on their bodies, and steam rose from their skin in the cool air. Leah licked her lips as she watched Ryder run a hand through his hair, the muscles in his arms bunching in all the right places. She couldn't wait to run her tongue down his abs to those sexy lines that carved his hips. She'd had her hands on him but hadn't done more than that since she'd been an idiot and wanted to go slow.

Her teeth bit into her lip as he bent over when the play began. He started off, running along his path until he turned at the right moment, catching the ball perfectly. He made it a few feet before Bram tackled him to the ground.

It might be touch football, but they were shifters so things got a bit...physical.

Dear goddess.

It felt good to laugh and play. Without being able to relieve the tension of the potential war and Unveiling, the Pack might falter. The upper levels of wolves seemed to understand that, and had brought in the younger wolves to play, as well. There were at least four games going on at once, including soccer, football, and Rugby, but Leah's attention was on the Brentwood versus Jamenson game that included a few friends, as well.

Ryder rolled to his feet and shook the snow from his hair. Leah held back a groan as his fingers danced over his abs to wipe away the dirt and moisture.

"Um...Leah?" Brie's voice sounded like it was holding back laughter, and Leah turned toward her new friend.

"What is it?" And why weren't the other woman watching their men?

"Look at your hands, honey," Brie said softly, this time ending on a laugh.

Brynn snorted, then threw her head back in a laugh, too. "Are the men making you...hot?"

Leah frowned and looked down at her hands. She let out a curse and her cheeks heated. She quickly pulled her hands away from the puddles of water on either side of her and shook them off.

"Oops." She tried to keep back a smile but couldn't help but laugh along with the other women.

"I'd ask if you were enjoying the show but..." Brie trailed off and wiggled her eyebrows.

"Apparently, I pulled in the snow from around us and uh...melted it." They'd purposely sat in a place without snow so they wouldn't end up too cold and wet, but her powers had pulled on that water like nobody's business.

"I didn't know you could melt things," Charlotte said as she came to their group. She sat down next to Leah after Leah had dried up the puddle for her.

"I can't melt things, but I can change the physical state of anything made of water."

"Good to know," Brie put in then let out another sigh. "I see now why you said we shouldn't join in today with the game," she said to Brynn.

Brynn rubbed her hands together in glee. "Oh, yeah. I mean, we play along most times since it's not a boys' club by any means, but I knew they'd be shirtless today...and in the snow." She let out another dreamy sigh. "Don't you just love the way the steam comes off their skin like that?"

Leah's mouth went dry as Ryder laughed at something Walker said. "Oh, yeah."

"Things going well with you and Ryder, then?" Charlotte asked, her focus on Bram. "Or at least better?"

She felt the gazes of the other two women on her but tried to ignore it. "I think." She pressed her lips together. "I don't know if I'm ready to talk about it yet."

"We're here if you need us," Brie said.

"Mating is hard," Brynn put in, her voice a little sad. "Harder than it should be sometimes." Brie took Brynn's hand and the women shared a look Leah didn't understand.

"We're not going to bond," Leah said, despite the fact that she'd just told them she wasn't ready to talk about it. But she didn't want the others to get the wrong impression. "That's not in the cards for us."

The other two frowned at her, and Charlotte squeezed her hand.

"It's okay," she lied. "Really. I'm here to help when the time comes, not to mate into the Pack. You know?" She blew out a breath. "Anyway, have you heard anything from the

Coven yet?" A change of subject was in order, even if it wasn't neatly done.

"No word," Brie answered. "Gideon thinks they are planning something, but he doesn't know what. It's been quiet on all fronts for a while."

"And that's a bit scary," Brynn put in. "The Redwoods are on edge." Brynn had mated into the Redwoods since Finn was the Heir.

"The Talons, too," Brie said. "Hence the football game. Though the women need to let off some steam, as well."

Brynn smiled. "I'm sure most of us will be able to in a certain fashion." The two women shared another look, and Leah met Charlotte's gaze.

The other woman didn't look sad at the fact that she wouldn't be going home with one of the wolves playing ball. Instead, she rolled her eyes. Leah wasn't sure what she'd be doing with Ryder once they were done with the game either.

Brynn let out a small growl as Finn hit the ground thanks to Mitchell. The Talon Beta just grinned at Brynn as he pulled Finn to his feet. Brynn stood up and raised her chin.

"Okay, so I'm still totally going to do my mate against a wall later, but now I want some blood." With that, she ran onto the field and held out her arms. "I'm playing. Get over it."

Leah just laughed as Brynn's brothers begged for her to be on their team, rather than the Redwoods. Finn took away that choice by pulling her to his side, his hand on her ass, and kissed her firmly on the lips.

Brie stood up and rolled her shoulders. "I might be a submissive wolf, but I'm going to kick some ass." She winked then ran over to her mate. Gideon, who had been holding the football because, of course, he was the quarterback, tossed the ball over his shoulder. Brandon caught it and laughed as Gideon gripped Brie's hips and lifted her off her feet. He kissed her hard and kept his hand on her butt as he laughed at something his mate said.

Leah met Charlotte's gaze and lifted her brows. "Should we?"

Charlotte just grinned and stood up, taking Leah's hand in hers. "Let's do it. But I'm going to kick your ass. Just saying."

They ran onto the field and Leah couldn't help but laugh. Ryder eyed her as she came to his side. He held out his hand and she took it, whatever tension she'd been holding onto about joining in on the game leaving her.

"Do you mind if I join?" she asked. She wasn't Pack and not a shifter. These guys could hit hard, and even though Brie was a submissive wolf, she was still much stronger than Leah.

"I don't mind at all," Ryder said. He studied her face. "We won't tackle you."

Max, Ryder's cousin, grinned as he came to Ryder's side. The other wolf made her smile every time she saw him. She couldn't help it. He was just so...happy.

"Well, we won't tackle you. Ryder might." He winked, and Leah just rolled her eyes.

Ryder let out a growl and kicked out, knocking his

cousin behind the knees. Max hit the ground on his side, but only laughed.

"Enough fun and games!" Gideon called out. "Let's play!"

"Oh, yes, because us playing football isn't fun at all," Brie said dryly.

He leaned down and bit her lip. "Watch it, woman." He smacked her ass again then lifted his chin.

Ryder pulled Leah to his side at the line of scrimmage and smiled. "There are way too many of us on the field at the moment, but just roll with it." He leaned down and whispered in her ear, his warm breath sending tingles down her neck. "Gideon's going to throw the ball to me. Stay behind me and I'll get it to you. You'll be my secret weapon."

She smiled up at him, feeling lighter than she'd ever felt before. "Sounds like a plan." And if she dropped the ball, she could always keep running.

Since they'd sort of made up the rules and amount of players on the field, as soon as Gideon caught the ball from Mitchell, Ryder took off. Leah ran behind him, chest heaving because, damn, the man could run. Ryder turned at the last moment and caught the ball perfectly.

Leah sucked in a breath as Finn and Quinn came barreling toward Ryder, then squealed as Ryder tossed the ball back to her.

"Run!"

She held the ball to her chest and ran as fast as she could. Give her a soccer ball or even a baseball bat, and she could kick ass. Give her a football, and, apparently, she wanted to fumble and giggle.

Cheers and shouts sounded behind her, but she tried to ignore them as she ran. As soon as she hit the end zone she slowed down and turned on her heel.

"I did it!" She laughed as Ryder picked her up by the hips and twirled her around.

"Knew you could, little witch." She held the ball in one hand over her head and wrapped her legs around his waist.

"Well, you did the catching," she said on a laugh.

Ryder grinned, then put his hand on the back of her neck and brought her head down to his. She let out a surprised gasp as he kissed her full-out in front of his family and friends.

She hadn't known he'd want to do that, and frankly, didn't know what it meant, but for now, she kissed him back and fell into the feel of his lips.

"And on that note, I think we're done," Mitchell said dryly from the side. "I'm going to go kick some of the youth's butts in soccer."

Ryder let her slide down his body and set her feet on the ground once Mitchell started to walk away. "You ready to head home? Or do you want to play another game?"

She met his gaze and studied his face. His wolf wasn't at the surface, which surprised her. This was Ryder asking, not his wolf.

"Let's go to your place."

It wasn't lost on her that he'd said home while she'd said his place. She was staying there while they made decisions and plans. She didn't live there. She didn't live anywhere. And thinking about that just annoyed her because she didn't normally feel so bad about her life. She lived it. She didn't dwell on it.

They said their goodbyes to the others as they either continued a new game or headed home to their places. It wasn't lost on her that couples were the ones that left together and the singles more than likely stayed to play. Charlotte walked away with Bram, but they kept a distance between them. While Leah wanted to know more so she could help her friend, she knew Charlotte would tell her when she was ready.

Ryder took her hand in his as he led her to his place. It wasn't until they were in his foyer that she realized she still held the football.

"Crap. I didn't mean to steal it."

Ryder took it from her and set it on the front table in the center. "We have others, and you deserve this one. You scored the winning touchdown, after all." He reached out and helped her with her coat, and she couldn't help the shiver as his fingers brushed her skin.

She licked her lips, then reached up and kissed his jaw. "Well, I couldn't have done it without you. Thank you for letting me play."

Ryder slid his hand through her hair and cupped the back of her head. "Thank you for wanting to." He let out a breath. "What am I going to do with you, little witch?"

"What do you want to do with me?"

He leaned down and rested his forehead on hers. "So fucking much, Leah. Too much."

Her heart hurt, the aching beat that should have been silent after what she'd promised herself. Her arms went numb at the thought of what would happen when she left him. Because he wouldn't be the one to leave her, as he'd never fully been there to begin with. He pushed her away even as he held her close, but she knew he had a reason. The fact that he didn't trust her with that reason broke her a bit each time her magic called to him, but she tried to not let it hurt her. She'd learned long ago that if she held herself back, if she hid part of herself, it didn't ache as badly.

He didn't trust her with the reason he couldn't mate with her, but he also couldn't keep his hands off of her. She couldn't fall for him because when it was time to go, it would only hurt that much more. So she would take what she could and give just as much. And then she'd walk away when it was time. This was just sex, just a...friend. And that was it. Nothing more. Nothing less.

And if she kept lying to herself, maybe she would believe it.

Her magic called to him. Her soul called to him.

And yet, he wouldn't have her.

So she would take him as he was and he would have to do the same. Because she wasn't ready for a mate, wasn't ready for that kind of sharing. The closer she got to another, the sharper the pain when someone betrayed her...or when she lost that someone.

"Leah," Ryder whispered. "Come back to me."

She blinked away her thoughts and tried to live in the moment. It was all she had, and she needed to relish it.

"Make love to me, Ryder," she said finally. "No promises. Just you and me."

He licked his lips, his eyes glowing gold. "Are you sure

that's what you want?"

No. But it was what she needed.

"Yes. Kiss me."

His thumb brushed her jaw and he nodded. "I can do that, Leah. I can do that and more."

When he lowered his lips to hers, she slid her hands around his hips and up his back, raking her nails ever so slightly along his skin. He hadn't put on a shirt during their short walk back from the field, and she'd never been so grateful. His skin was sweat-slick, and yet all she wanted to do was lick up his body and taste every curve. There had to be something wrong with her if she had that thought on her brain.

Ryder's mouth devoured hers, his tongue taking over, and she melted into him. When his hands went to her ass, she rocked against him and moaned. He cupped her, lifting her off the ground in a show of strength that shouldn't have surprised her, but did.

"I love your muscles," she blurted.

Ryder grinned, his eyes gold and sparkling. "I'll make sure to put them to work, then." He carried her to the bedroom as she wrapped her legs around his waist, his cock sitting perfectly against her clit. All she had to do was rock against him and maybe she'd come. But from the look in Ryder's eyes, if she did that, he might punish her.

Of course, she might like that just as much.

She slid down his front when they entered the bedroom and kissed his chest as she put her feet firmly on the floor. Ryder tangled his fingers in her hair and forced her gaze to his.

"I'm going to taste you, every inch of you, then I'm going to fuck you hard. So hard we're both spent and panting." He met her gaze and an odd look passed across his face. "We're going to use condoms, Leah. Be sure."

She knew what he meant. There were two steps to every mating. The first was sex where the man would come within their mate, cementing their bond on the human end. The second was a mating mark where the wolf in human form would bite into the other's shoulder. In a case of two wolves mating, each would do it, but she'd heard that even humans and witches who mated into the Pack bit down because of the emotional connections. That mark signified the mating between the wolf and the other in a way that spoke of magic and the goddess.

A condom would prevent the first step, and he'd made no mention of the mating mark since it wouldn't be a problem. It was a reminder that he would not mate her, but would take her. But she was giving herself freely, so was he really taking? She was going into this with eyes wide open, knowing even if he'd wanted to mate with her, she didn't want to tie her life to his.

Instead of answering, she reached around him and gripped his ass before kissing down his chest. He seemed to take that in stride and ran his hands down her back and then around her hips and back up again so he could cup her breasts. He'd made her come before, but she'd never seen him naked, and she'd never been fully bare in front of him.

They were taking the next step—maybe not the step they should have been taking—but it was step they understood.

He went to his knees in front of her and tugged on the bottom of her shirt. She helped him lift it over her head, then sucked in her lip as he licked and nibbled up her belly and toward her breasts. She wasn't that tall, and he was damn big, so she only had to lean over for him to be able to bite at her breasts through her bra. When she reached around and undid the clasp, he let out an approving growl. At least, she hoped it was approving because it made her wet just thinking about it.

He lifted the cups from her breasts then let out another growl. "Holy goddess, your nipples are fucking perfect. Like little ripe berries begging for my tongue."

She usually wasn't a fan of dirty talk, but if he were going to talk like that to her while licking at her nipples, then she'd take it. His other hand worked on the button of her jeans as he sucked her nipple into his mouth and she ran her hand through his hair, wanting more.

He pulled away then tugged on her jeans. "Off." His voice was more wolf than man.

She helped him take off her pants, then gasped as he nuzzled her pussy through her panties.

"You smell so fucking delicious. I'm going to eat your cunt, Leah. You ready for that? You ready for my tongue inside you and on your clit? I want you to come on my face until you can't breathe, and then I'm going to fuck you hard into the bed."

Holy hell. She almost came at his words alone.

"Get on the edge of the bed and take off your panties. Slowly."

He stood up as he spoke and worked on his pants.

"And what are you going to do when I take off my panties?" Even as she said it, she went to sit on the edge of the bed. She slowly slid her hands along her hips and around the edges of the lace, then even slower, slid them down her thighs, lifting her ass slightly so she could take them off.

His gaze was on her pussy, not her face, and she couldn't help but feel empowered that she'd done that to him, this strong, quiet wolf.

Ryder shucked off his jeans and boxer briefs, leaving him naked and hard. His cock stood at attention, thick and long and so rigid that she was afraid he might come right then. Instead, he fisted himself, giving his dick a few quick thrusts as he licked his lips.

"All the way off, Leah. Now."

She tossed her panties to the side, and feeling powerful, spread herself for him. He let out a groan and she slid her hand down her belly and over her clit.

"Like this?"

Ryder was on his knees in a flash, his face buried between her legs and his beard scraping along the skin of her inner thighs. He lapped at her, using his fingers to tease her until her body shook and she gasped for breath.

He growled low, the vibrations going straight to her clit, and she came, calling his name. Before she could blink, she was flat on her back and Ryder hovered above her. His condom-clad cock pressed against her opening as he stared intently into her eyes.

"You ready, little witch?"

"Goddess, yes."

He smiled before thrusting hard. Her eyes rolled to the back of her head and she tried to call out his name but couldn't formulate the word. Instead, she wrapped her arms around his biceps as he pounded into her, his cock stretching her yet relieving an ache she didn't know she'd had.

Ryder kissed her then, bringing her back to him as he made love to her, hard, fast, and thrilling. Her breasts pressed against his chest, her nipples hard and aching. When she met his gaze, her heart pounding for more than one reason, he pulled out and gripped her hips. She felt empty at the loss but soon found herself on her stomach with her face practically pressed into the mattress as he fucked her from behind. Her toes barely reached the floor, but he kept her steady, pounding into her. She bit into the sheets so she wouldn't call out, and her fingers gripped the cotton so hard she was afraid she'd tear it.

When he reached around and slid his fingers over her clit, she came again at his touch, this time with him as he filled the condom within her.

She came down from her high faster this time, aware she'd been thoroughly fucked and had come without looking at him—without him having to see her.

Leah knew why he'd done it. Not only had it been hot and an awesome position, but it had also kept a distance between them that was needed. He hadn't looked at her when he'd come and she'd been grateful. Because if he had seen her as she'd come again, he'd have seen too much.

And she was afraid she might not have seen enough.

CHAPTER
EIGHT

Ryder was a fucking idiot. He'd let his demons win, but there hadn't been another option.

You're nothing.

You're tainted.

Ryder closed his eyes and let his uncle's voice wash over him. The bastard had beaten him almost to death in life and now taunted him in death. One day, he might be able to push out the demons that plagued him, but he wasn't sure he'd ever find the way. It wasn't as if he knew of another wolf who had the same so-called powers as he did. As far as he knew, he was the only one.

That wasn't all that uncommon, however. He knew of a few Redwood wolves who held special powers. Such as Bay Jamenson. She had the ability to glean the histories of certain objects just by her touch. She could actually see the past wrapped around a pocket watch or random antique.

Her mating with Adam over thirty years ago had only heightened her senses.

And that was something Ryder couldn't allow to happen.

If he were to mate with another, he might increase the number of voices he heard, or worse, intensify the voices' power over him. He could even pass it on to his mate, as Maddox and Ellie had found out when the former Redwood Pack Omega mated with her.

He couldn't allow Leah to lose any more of herself by mating with him.

Hence why Ryder was a fucking idiot.

He'd never felt as alive as when he was deep inside Leah, lying to himself that making love to her was only because of the need and not something more. When he'd been on top of her, sliding in and out and having to hold onto that bare thread of control, he'd felt his fangs elongate, ready to mark, ready to claim.

His wolf had needed to mate, and Ryder couldn't allow that to happen.

So he'd pulled out of her and forced her onto her stomach so he could bring them both to completion without having to make eye contact. He hadn't wanted her to see the truth in his eyes—the truth that told her he wanted so much more than a hard fuck at the end of the day.

He wanted a true mating. Wanted someone he could share his life with. Wanted to form a mating bond that would heal them both from the inside out.

But that couldn't happen so he'd had to be an asshole.

After he'd pulled out of her and disposed of the condom, he'd spooned behind her, unable to be as crass as to leave her spent in the middle of the bed, alone and shaking. She hadn't looked behind her but had wrapped her hand around his as he cupped her breast. They'd slept like that without another word, but when he'd woken up early the next morning, he'd needed to leave her.

He'd wanted to wake her up by sweetly making love to her and kissing every inch of her skin. He'd wanted to show her that she was worth more than a damaged wolf.

As he couldn't do any of that, he'd left her a note on his pillow and gone for a run.

His body still ached from the exertion, the bones in his body not quite settled since he'd shifted as quickly as he could. He'd needed the pain to help tone down the desire running through his veins. Maybe if it hurt enough, he'd be able to forget who lay in his bed.

Ryder ran a hand through his hair before leaning against a tree, his chest hurting from either the strain of the run or what he'd done—maybe both. The sun slid through the clouds, warming his flesh; though he would have thought he'd be warm enough already with all the exercise he'd just done. He stood in the middle of the forest on Talon Pack land, safe enough behind the wards, and as alone as he could be.

As the Pack had made it a command that members come home and stay within the wards to be safe unless needed elsewhere, it was getting a bit crowded. If what his brother Kameron, the Enforcer, said was true, it might get even more crowded soon. It seemed Washington had a bill on the table that would force those of non-human nature to remain behind the wards for the long term.

Caged.

Forgotten.

Ryder didn't doubt that Kameron was right about those details, as it was his job as Enforcer to know about outside forces threatening the Pack. But that didn't mean Ryder wanted to deal with the outcome. He would, though. As always.

He took a deep breath and froze.

Two spirits slid toward him, their eyes blank, but every once in a while they would blink and he would see the agony that lay beneath.

He'd seen these spirits before—had seen them when they were alive, as well. And, of course, he'd seen them when they died.

They were two of his uncles—the former Enforcer and Healer. Their Pack hadn't had an Omega when his father was Alpha, and that was something unheard of for most Packs. Wolves could usually remain a healthy Pack without a Healer or Enforcer, but the Omegas were critical. The spirits of Uncle Reggie, the Healer, and Uncle Abraham, the Enforcer, stared at him, their mouths open, but no sound escaping.

They looked as if they were yelling, but he couldn't hear a damn thing.

He never could with them.

They misted toward him, not walking, but not really gliding either. He couldn't explain it, but it creeped him the hell out every time he saw it. At least, when Uncle Timothy appeared, he'd yell at Ryder, call him names, and actually announce his presence. Though, in reality, Ryder couldn't see Timothy as he could the others.

Or maybe it was that his abusive uncle didn't want Ryder to see him—just another form of torture and abuse.

It killed him each time he heard his uncle's voice in his head. It wasn't as if he could block it out or fully ignore it. His uncle would just get louder and scream until he finally acknowledged the bastard.

What made it all worse, was that the former Beta, Timothy, had treated all of Ryder's siblings and cousins with respect. He'd acted as if he loved them and tried to care for the wounds inflicted by the other uncles.

Yet as soon as the curtains were drawn, he'd torture and beat Ryder until Ryder passed out from the pain. The other uncles had known what was going on. Through the bonds, they couldn't hide it for long, even with how broken that hierarchy had been.

When they'd died, and Ryder and his siblings were burdened with the mantle instead, he hadn't had the heart to tell the others that the one uncle who had shown them compassion was actually just as bad as the rest. If not worse.

So he'd hid his past from them, from everyone.

He hid his abilities, his scars, and now, he would hide what he felt for Leah. It was the only way to keep the others' memories safe. He'd do anything for them.

Ryder's pulse pounded in his temples and he closed his eyes. He tried to take a deep breath, only to come up short as his skin went icy cold. He shivered as the two spirits slid through him, moving past him on their way to wherever the hell they stayed when they weren't bothering him.

It felt as if someone had walked over his grave before trying to drown him in icy water.

His arms shook and his legs threatened to give out from under him, but the spirits' presence and touch only strengthened his resolve to stay away from Leah. She didn't deserve this. She didn't deserve a broken mate, and she sure as hell didn't deserve any special powers he might possess that could be passed on to her. It might not be a sure thing that she'd end up with them, but since it was an option at all, he wouldn't—couldn't—allow it.

"I wish you would tell me what's wrong," Brandon said as he came close.

Ryder hadn't scented his brother, hadn't felt him near. His damn wolf had been useless, but then again, his brother had come from downwind and had probably purposely done his best to hide his scent.

Damn freaking Omega.

"I'm fine," Ryder bit out through clenched teeth.

"You're lying."

Ryder opened his eyes and growled. He let his wolf come to the surface and knew his eyes were glowing gold. "Fuck off."

Brandon studied his face and frowned. "There's something off with you, something I've always sensed even before I was the Omega, but I can't figure it out. You're in pain, Ryder. Let me help."

Let the little weakling help. Show him how useless you are.

His uncle whispered in his ear and Ryder growled, his hands fisting at his sides.

"Ryder. What's wrong?"

"It's none of your damn business," Ryder snapped.

"You're my brother, and I'm the Omega," Brandon said softly, patiently. Bastard. "It's my job to care for the Pack."

His uncle kept whispering in one ear and the two spirits from before came back, sliding over Ryder's skin like ice water. His wolf raged, and Ryder needed to lash out.

Only there wasn't anyone alive in front of him who deserved it. Only Brandon.

"Get off your fucking high horse and go away. I don't need your fucking emo powers."

"Ryder."

He growled again then struck. His fist connected with Brandon's jaw before he'd thought better of it. Brandon might be soft-spoken and kind, but he was still a wolf, and a challenge like this couldn't be ignored. His brother hit back, slamming into Ryder's side. Ryder lowered his head and let a low rumble come from his chest.

"No fangs. No claws."

Brandon nodded then sprang. Ryder ducked out of the way, rolling to the ground before coming back to his bare feet. He kicked out, knocking into Brandon's knee. His brother faltered for a minute before taking out Ryder's legs instead. The two wrestled on the ground, throwing punches that connected more often than not. His wolf reveled in it, loving the feel of another wolf to play with, as well as a way to let out his aggression.

"What are you doing?" Leah's voice came to him as he straddled Brandon, his fist ready to punch again. Only he'd frozen as soon as he heard her and hadn't been able to protect his face.

Brandon's fist landed on his nose, the resounding crunch an echo between his ears. Blood spurted, and he cursed, covering his face before stumbling to his feet.

Brandon let out another curse and gingerly stood up. "Fuck. I didn't mean to break it."

Ryder winced, the pain not too bad; he'd had far worse. But he hadn't been prepared for it, so it hurt like a bitch.

"Oh, goddess, you're bleeding. Well, both of you are, but Ryder, your nose." Leah came up to him, stripping off her cardigan as she did. She held it out, and he took it without thinking. "Put it against your nose to sop up the blood." He did as he was told because she'd asked it of him. As soon as he did, he wanted to growl. Now he had her scent pressed up against his face and he had to deal with a hard-on as well as whatever the hell was going on with him.

"I'm fine," he said, a bit muffled.

"No, you aren't." Leah sighed. "Neither one of you are. What is wrong with you? Why were you fighting?"

Ryder shrugged. "Just blowing off steam."

Brandon mumbled an assent. "We're fine, Leah. He's had his nose broken by at least one of us before. We're wolves."

Leah mumbled something about barbaric men and stupid practices but kept her hand on his arm. He hadn't realized she'd touched him, but he should have. He was hard and confused as hell. Damn it. He'd run to get her out of his system, and now he had her scent on his face and her hand on his body.

The exact opposite of what he needed.

"We have a meeting with the Coven in an hour. Are you going to be okay to go?"

Ryder pulled her cardigan away from his face and raised a brow at her. "I'll be healed in twenty minutes, Leah. I just need to clean up the blood." He winced when he looked down at what she'd given him. "I think I've ruined this, though."

"It stopped the blood, so whatever. Now, come on, let me make sure you didn't break anything else." She turned to Brandon. "Do you need to come with us?"

Ryder's wolf pressed up against him, not liking that idea one bit.

Brandon shook his head, his eyes on Ryder. "I'm okay. I didn't have anything broken."

"Lucky punch," Ryder snarled.

"I'm just that good." With that, his brother walked off, but Ryder suspected he'd done what he'd set out to do. Ryder may not have spilled his secrets, but he felt a little better by letting out some of his aggression. Damn it. He might have to thank Brandon now.

"I don't understand men," Leah muttered.

Ryder leaned down and kissed her forehead. He knew he shouldn't, but he couldn't help it. "We're simple creatures. We like fighting. Women. And booze."

She rolled her eyes but slid her hand in his as they made their way to his place. He didn't know what he was going to do about her, but damn it, he'd just have to deal. Somehow. He always had before.

———

LEAH WANTED to bury her head in the sand and forget everything around her, but that wouldn't be helpful in the slightest. Two hours into the Coven meeting, and they were no better off than they had been when they'd walked in. At least the name-calling had stopped.

"That witch is the reason we're in this mess. A mongrel," her father spat.

Ah, the name-calling was back it seemed.

"Luis," one of the other witches whispered. "Please. Using those names gets us nowhere."

Considering the fact that the man had slept with her mother and was, therefore, part of her whole genetic makeup, calling her a mongrel was bad form. Not that the man ever cared about that.

She might technically be the bastard, but he was the one who acted like one.

Ryder squeezed her thigh, and she looked over at him. "I'm fine," she whispered. "He can't hurt me." A lie, as the man could hurt her with each word, and perhaps even more with his actions, but she would at least try not to let it hurt."

"Witches are burning, and we're here discussing politics," Luis snarled. "There is blame to be laid, and we have the culprit right in front of us." She felt his gaze on her and turned toward him, her chin raised.

"Are we back to this?" Finn Jamenson asked, frustration

clear in his tone. "The witches and wolves are now in the public eye, and there's nothing we can do to stop that. Putting blame on the victim is only hampering our efforts."

"She's the one that did her magic on camera. She's no victim." Her father glared at her, and she was pretty sure he'd end her if he had the chance. There would be no happy reunion with this man. Not that there had ever been a chance of that. He'd tried to have her wiped off the face of the earth before she'd even been born, and had his henchman after her family ever since he'd failed. He hadn't wanted tainted blood out in the world, and now he couldn't do anything about it without endangering the wolves.

She wouldn't put it past him to try, though.

At that sobering thought, she'd had enough. "I was only protecting myself and my brother," she put in and cursed herself. She hated being the center of attention, and now it seemed she'd never get out of it.

"Enough," Ryder growled. "This is getting us nowhere. We need to iron out the details of not only our treaty, but the public face of what is to come. The humans are after us. Not all of them, of course, but many in power. And don't forget, the witches you see burning are not being killed by those in power, but by those who feel they don't have enough. Do you not understand that? The ones that feel as though they are being subjugated and oppressed with each new Unveiling are the ones lashing out first. They don't have to think of the consequences because they feel they are right. They are killing wolves and witches because they feel as though they are doing a service by taking out so-called lesser beings."

"And it's not just them," Leah added, encouraged by Ryder's words. He didn't often speak to others, but when he did, it was because he had something to say. "The Coven and other smaller covens around the area are safe for now because they are in hiding as much as possible. Packs around the U.S. are still in hiding unless they've been forced into the public eye like the Redwoods and Talons. We're far greater in number than the humans know, and that is creating fear on both sides. If we don't stand together, we will fall apart."

The room grew quiet after her and Ryder's speeches before they began to once again try to formulate a plan. She knew the Alphas of the Packs had their own plans and were purposely not present at these meetings. She also knew the Coven had probably had meetings, as well. However, something good had to come of this. It had to.

Only she wasn't sure it could happen if she were in the room for much longer. While the Talons had asked her to be there so they had a witch on their side, she wasn't the only witch they knew. Hannah and Gina were also there in the back of the room, listening to everything unfold. She let out a sigh, and Ryder looked down at her. He took her hand and leaned toward her.

"What's wrong?"

She blinked up at him and did her best to not lean forward and kiss him. Not only would it be stupid to do that in front of his family and Pack as they weren't on the path to mating, but doing so in front of the Coven would only heighten the tension in the room. If they thought she was only there because she'd slept with one of the Talon Pack members, she'd be called a whore just as they'd called her mother one.

Her mother might not have known Luis was married at the time, but it hadn't mattered when Darynda and the other witches cast their blame of the whole situation on her mother's shoulders rather than Luis's.

Just thinking about the past made her angry. She needed to think of the future—at least the welfare of the Pack and any innocent witches. Her own future was far murkier, and she would prefer not to think about that at all.

"I need some air," she whispered. "I'll be right back." As quietly as she could, she pushed her chair back and made her way from the table. The witches glared at her, and the wolves looked worried, but she shook her head and pointed to the door. Odd that it was those unlike her in genetics, the wolves, who had her back while those who should have opened their arms to her pushed her away.

She made her way to the door, but Hannah and Gina followed her. She smiled at them, wishing she knew them better. They were both witches who lived within wolf dens. There were more than just these two, but they were the ones she knew a bit more because of their hierarchy within the Redwood Pack.

As soon as she stepped outside, she inhaled the fresh scent of the outdoors and immediately felt a little better. Not at peace, but at least not constantly on edge. Bram from the Redwoods, and Ryder's cousin, Max stood guard outside. They both looked at her expectantly, and she shook her head.

"I'm fine. Everything is going...well, not good, but at least they aren't throwing things. I just needed air."

Max smiled at her, and she couldn't help but smile back. Bram nodded silently then went back to keeping an eye on the perimeter.

"You doing okay?" Hannah asked when she came to Leah's side. "I know that was a lot in there, and I'm surprised you didn't smack a few of them. As it was, I had to keep my magic in check."

"I'm fine," Leah said. "I mean, I'm not going to be invited to any family reunions anytime soon, but the glares and accusations are better than outright offensive magic directed my way."

"That sucks, hon," Gina said softly. "I grew up within the Redwoods and never had to deal with a coven. My mother, my birth mother that is, mated into the Pack and left her small coven behind. Apparently, there wasn't any love lost there. My younger brother Mark and I learned what we could from her magic-wise before she died. And my adoptive mother did her best to help, as well, though she grew up in the human world without knowing about our secrets at all."

Leah knew Gina had been adopted by Kade and Melanie, the Alphas of the Redwoods years ago and had eventually mated a Talon wolf named Quinn. Since Gina was now the Enforcer of the Redwoods, Quinn had left the Talons to be with her. He'd also taken his son from a previous mating with him.

Leah had been with the Talons for long enough that she

sort of understood the Pack dynamics, but she wasn't sure she would ever get it all straight.

"I'm wolf and I am witch," Gina continued. "So I never had to deal with the idea of mating into the Pack in order to keep my long life. I know some witches prefer to change into wolf instead of being one or the other in order to keep their lives long, especially if they were adopted into the Pack and not mated. Witches have the same lifespan as humans without the mating bond. With the mating bond, witches can live as long as their mate does, like Hannah. But humans need to change to wolves—a process that almost kills them, in order to stay long-lived with their mates."

"I didn't grow up with a coven either," Hannah added. "My mother and I chose to open our herb and oil shop and just live as witches in the real world. The humans just thought it was our religion, or maybe that we were just eccentric." Hannah winked. "I guess none of us had a normal witch upbringing, and now we're living amongst the wolves."

Leah sighed. "I don't know how much longer I'll be with the Talons, though," Leah said honestly. "I don't know if I'm a help or a hindrance. I don't want to stay there if I'll only cause problems."

Hannah turned to her sharply. "But I thought...you and Ryder..."

Leah shook her head. "We're choosing not to mate." Goddess, why did that hurt to say? It shouldn't. It was a rational decision. Ryder didn't want to burden her with... whatever secret he held close, and she didn't want to put a bull's-eye on his back by mating him. It was better for both of them if they stayed apart.

And if she kept telling herself that, maybe it would make sense.

Gina pressed her lips together but didn't say anything.

"I'm sorry," Hannah whispered. "I didn't mean to bring up such a sore subject. These days, there only seems to be those kinds of subjects, though."

Leah snorted. "Pretty much. I can't walk without running into an issue from the past, or one that isn't quite finished in the present."

"That's the problem when you have centuries to live," Gina said. "Lots of layers of history and not everyone is willing to share it."

Leah ran a hand over her face. She opened her mouth to say something, only to come up short. The ground beneath her feet shook as a bomb—it had to be a bomb—went off near them.

Gina pulled Hannah under her as she dropped to the ground since the Enforcer was wolf and could handle most damage, while Hannah was only a witch. A witch like Leah. But Leah was too far away for Gina to protect with her strength. Another bomb went off, and Leah fell to her knees, the force of the impact in the air too much.

Bram and Max ran toward her but were thrown from their feet as another bomb went off. Leah pulled on her magic, trying to find out what was going on and figure out how to fix it; only she couldn't concentrate. Her ears rang and her head pounded. Hands grabbed at her roughly, and she tried to fight; only she couldn't. Something sharp pricked her neck, and she screamed. A hand went over her mouth, and her body felt heavy.

She tried to blink, tried to do something to save herself; only she couldn't think enough to function.

She succumbed to the darkness with one thought on her mind.

Ryder.

CHAPTER

NINE

The walls shook as what sounded like a bomb went off right outside the building. Ryder was on his feet in an instant, adrenaline coursing through his veins. His wolf raged, clawing at him to shift so they could find their mate and bring her to safety.

Leah.

Had she been outside when the bomb went off?

Shit.

He inhaled; the scent of burnt diesel and chemicals filled his nostrils and he coughed, trying to expel the odor. He ran toward the door as fast as he could. His family and the Redwoods followed him, their wolves in their eyes.

It was no surprise to him that most of the witches ran toward the other door in the room. The one away from the bomb. A few witches followed Ryder and his crew, worry in their eyes, but their hands raised to use magic. There was even a pregnant witch who looked like she wanted to follow, but someone pulled her back. Ryder didn't blame them for wanting the woman safe. She had to protect her young. However, he could blame all the other able-bodied witches who didn't want to see if their own security team outside was safe.

Or perhaps they knew they were safe and this was all a ploy.

"Finn," he called out.

Finn met his gaze and seemed to be on the same track. "Fuck. Got it. I'll go with them. Just to make sure. Drake, with me." The two ran after the witches to make sure they weren't going to run off, in case they were the ones responsible, but he hoped to the goddess they wouldn't be hurt in the process. The sheer fact that Finn had trusted his Redwood wolves out front with Ryder spoke volumes.

Ryder made his way through the final door and out into the chaos. Another bomb went off close to the compound, and he was thrown back into the wall, Brandon right next to him. His ears rang, but he just shook his head and staggered to his feet. He was pretty sure he had a few cuts all over his exposed skin thanks to flying debris, but he didn't care. He needed to find Leah and the rest of his Packmates before it was too late.

As soon as he took a few steps, he spotted Gina on the ground, covering another person. From the curly brown hair covered in a layer of debris and dust, he figured the woman beneath Gina had to be Hannah. Brandon took off running and Ryder followed him.

"Gina!" he called out. He didn't know where the enemy was, and with all the smoke and broken ground and trees around them, he couldn't get a scent lock on the bastards. For all he knew, this was like the last time the Talon Pack had been bombed by human extremists. They'd used timed devices that could go off without anyone having to be near.

How they—whoever they were—knew the witches and wolves were meeting there was a question that would have to be answered.

Soon.

But first, he needed Leah and his Pack.

The fact that he thought of Leah first in all situations was not lost on him, but he'd have to deal with that later. Instead, he slid beside Gina and pulled her off Hannah.

"Let's go. We need to get away from here." His voice was firm, but he didn't make it a true order. She wasn't his Pack, and though he was more dominant than her, he didn't want to use it and cause Pack issues. He fucking hated politics sometimes.

Gina lifted her head and met his gaze. A few cuts marred her face, but she didn't look much worse for wear. She let out a little growl, but he didn't feel that it was directed at him. "Every time I tried to move toward some-place safer, they let off another freaking bomb." Brandon stepped closer to her, but she held him off. Ryder didn't think the action was rude, just two friends who needed their space after a harrowing ordeal.

"It makes using magic a bit difficult when you're trying not to hurt your Pack and you have no idea where to aim," Hannah said dryly as Ryder lifted her into his arms. "I can walk just fine," she snapped but put her arms around his neck. As she had two very dominant mates, he had a feeling she was used to wolves carrying her around when there was danger. She was a tiny witch that might be able to Heal others, but she couldn't Heal herself.

He set Hannah down on her feet near the building and away from where most of the bombs had gone off. They wouldn't be completely safe until they were behind the den wards, but it would have to do for now. Brandon came closer and looked over her cuts, but as they didn't have a first aid kit on them, it didn't do much good.

"Have you seen Leah?" he asked, his wolf frantic. Hell, he was frantic, too.

Hannah's eyes widened and she looked behind him. "She was right by us when the first bomb went off. We all hit the ground and Gina covered me."

Gina cursed. "Hannah was closer to me." She met Ryder's eyes. "I couldn't reach Leah. I'm sorry."

He would have liked to blame Gina for not covering his mate, but he couldn't. And he needed to stop fucking thinking about her as his mate. She was not. But she was his, if only for the moment.

"Stay here with Hannah," he growled. "Finn is around the back with the other witches. I'm going to find Leah."

"Max and Bram are around here, as well," Hannah said. "Be careful, Ryder. We don't know who is out there. And don't forget, I might not be able to heal like you, but I can still protect myself." She raised her chin and he lowered his gaze in acknowledgement. She was right. Her powers were far stronger than any other witch he'd met. He'd just seen her on the ground and assumed the worst.

He left the two to protect themselves and find the others

while he and Brandon went in search of Leah. It had been a few minutes since the last bomb, but that didn't mean there wouldn't be another one soon. As he searched, he shot off a quick text to his Alpha, letting him know what was going on. He wasn't sure what the next step would be, but he did know that if he didn't find Leah soon, he wouldn't be responsible for his actions.

"Ryder!" Bram called out.

He turned toward the other wolf and cursed. Bram had Max's arm around his shoulder and was practically dragging his cousin toward the compound.

"What happened?" He took Max's other side and helped the progress. Bram could have easily lifted him since he was a wolf, but Max was just tall enough that it would have been awkward as hell. Brandon came up behind them, his body on alert in case the enemy was near.

"Bomb blew too close and the damn wolf pushed me out of the way," Bram gritted out. "Knocked him out cold. He's still breathing, and he should be fine soon I would think. But I'd get him to your Healer just in case."

"Damn cousin," Ryder muttered.

An SUV pulled in next to him and Ryder let his claws out, his wolf on edge. When Hannah opened the passenger door and ran toward him, he relaxed somewhat.

"Get him in the back," she ordered. "I might not be a Healer for the Talons, but I can at least do what I can." She met Max's gaze. "We'll get him to Walker. Your brother will be able to help him."

Ryder nodded and helped Max into the back of the SUV.

He was trusting his blood with the Redwoods, and yet he knew it was the right decision.

Gina had her window down as the car idled. "Finn and Drake are taking care of the other witches, though they claim they weren't part of it." She let out a snort. "I don't know as I truly believe that. This is a bit too much of a coincidence, and I know our Packs didn't do it." She cursed. "But Finn can't actually keep them there for long."

Brandon let out a curse of his own. "He can try his best, but yeah, we don't have proof. And frankly, this could have been the humans finding us on their own."

"And we're sure the bombers are humans?" Ryder asked, his mind on the fact that they still hadn't found Leah.

"I scented humans near us right as the bomb blew," Gina said. "But before I could do anything about it, I was knocked to the ground."

"Get Max to my brother," Ryder said, his wolf at the forefront. If he didn't control it better, he'd shift right there and tear into the next thing that moved. "I'm going to find Leah."

"I'm going with you," Brandon said then turned on his heel. He and Ryder ran back to where Gina had said she saw Leah last and searched the area.

Ryder couldn't scent a damn thing and it was killing him. "I can't fucking scent her."

Brandon let out a breath and knelt on the grass to get a closer look. "I can't either. Whatever they put in the explosives added extra scents to them I think. Ones to mess with our senses."

"Fuck. That means they were not only aiming to kill us,

but to hamper our recovery. Fucking humans." He pushed at his wolf again, keeping his control on a thin leash. He couldn't shift, not yet.

"Damn it, Ryder," Brandon muttered.

Ryder turned to his brother and knelt beside him. "What is it?"

Brandon gingerly held up a small syringe between two fingers. "It has Leah's scent on the needle."

Ryder blinked once, twice, at the syringe, then threw his head back and howled. The mournful sound ended on a growl, and he had to take deep breaths so he didn't do something stupid like run in a random direction to search for her.

"We need to find her, Brandon. The fact they took her isn't a coincidence. Nothing is adding up."

"Let's spread out and find her scent trail," Finn said as he came up behind them.

Ryder stood quickly and turned to the other man. He fisted his hands at his sides and tried to calm his rapid breathing. "They took her, Finn," he bit out.

Finn reached out slowly and put his hand on Ryder's shoulder. His wolf calmed somewhat, and Ryder's eyes widened.

"You're not my Pack, how did you do that?"

"Your wolf just needed another dominant wolf to be there. It's not magic. Now take another deep breath and think. You can't find Leah if you're going off half-cocked. We will find her scent trail buried beneath the shit they pumped into the air. Once we do, we'll follow it and find her."

What wasn't said was the fact that he hadn't claimed Leah. He'd purposely tried to keep that distance, and now he couldn't use the mating bond to try and find her. Though they'd slept together, her scent was buried beneath his skin. His past issues might have hampered his ability to find her. Fuck.

"We can't kill humans," Brandon added and kept his chin up as Ryder growled at him. "We're still trying to act like we're happy wolves that protect their own. I'm not saying we can't rough them up for taking her, but the authorities might want to get involved. We still have to straddle that line until we know what laws are coming. Gutting the assholes where they stand might be what is needed, but we can't."

Ryder closed his eyes and prayed for patience. It didn't matter that Brandon was right. He wanted Leah. That was all. After that, he'd deal with everyone else.

"Fine. We find Leah. Then you deal with the fucking humans. I can't make any promises."

They went off in separate directions, each taking a small section of the surrounding area in hopes of catching her scent. All the while, his wolf raged and his mind whirled. If he'd left Leah at the den, this wouldn't have happened. If he'd mated with her, it might have been easier to find her. If he hadn't let her leave the room and kept her by his side, she might not have been taken. If he...

If.

All ifs.

And no action.

"Ryder!" Bram called out from his left.

"Ryder!" Finn called out from his right.

He cursed and went toward Bram since he'd heard him first. "What is it?" he asked the other wolf.

Sweat glistened on the wolf's dark skin and Bram let out a breath. "I caught her scent here. But Finn just texted and said he found her scent on another trail."

Ryder cursed. "They must have taken her jacket or some shit and tried to catch us off guard and confuse us. They know far too much about wolves."

"We're out in the open now," Bram said. "People want to find out everything they can about us. And now the same with witches." He put his phone up to his ear as it buzzed, and Ryder tilted his head so he could hear the conversation. Sometimes having enhanced senses helped.

"I say we split up," Finn said. "We each follow the trail and call the others as soon as we can if we find something. We're stronger together, but we're not weak apart."

"I agree," Ryder said. He didn't have to speak loudly for the other man to hear as they were all wolves and privacy on a phone conversation wasn't an option.

Both of them were Heirs and were in charge of the other wolves since neither Alpha was around. They, of course, would let their Pack know what was going on, and had been doing so already, but waiting for Gideon to come to him wasn't an option. He didn't want to think about how scared Leah must be. Hell, he didn't want to think about the alternative to her being scared and alive. He wasn't sure he could bear it.

"Drake and I will go this way. Brandon and Bram can go with you, Ryder, as they are closer to you."

They all agreed and made their plans before Bram hung up. Brandon had already made his way to them and the three set out to follow her scent. He prayed that they were on the right trail because he wasn't sure what he'd do if he lost Leah. It was already a form of torture to be near her and have her in his bed but not have her. It was a mess of his own making, but damn it, he couldn't lose her. Not like this.

They made their way in silence, on alert and ready to fight. He didn't know exactly how much of a head start the humans had, or if they had vehicles, but the three of them were running as fast as they could without making a sound. They remained human in case they came upon a non-friendly, but fuck, he wanted to shift and tear the faces off the humans who dared to touch her.

Ryder inhaled again and slowed down. He held up his hand, and Bram and Brandon came to his side. He tilted his head and tried to see if he could hear anything other than the normal sounds of leaves rustling and animals in the forest. However, he could scent the presence of humans. Not many, but enough in a place that there weren't normally a group of them that it gave him pause. It could be a group of hikers that had gone deep into the national forest, or it could be those who'd taken his Leah.

He could hear a few men speaking in hushed tones and the sound of metal against metal. The scent of gun oil reached his nose and he held back a curse. These had to be the assholes who had Leah. Either that, or they were hunters in the wrong part of the forest. It wouldn't be the first time, but hell, Leah's trail led here. This had to be them.

He opened his mouth to say something, but two spirits

slid out of the trees and stared at him. They didn't scream or try to touch him. Instead, the unfamiliar ghosts came closer and nodded at him before turning in the direction of the humans. He narrowed his eyes at them then blinked. Wait. He'd seen these two before. They were two of the apparitions he'd seen around the Coven. The spirits he'd assumed were ancestor witches. And now, they seemed to be pointing him in the right direction without asking for anything from him. He didn't understand it.

They nodded again at him, and he studied them, noticing that they were a man and a woman in older robes. The woman had Leah's eyes. She wasn't Leah's mother, as this woman looked far older than the woman would have been when she died, but Ryder would bet this ghost was an ancestor of Leah's. Whether on Luis's side or her mother's, he wasn't sure, but it was clear that these two spirits wanted to help as much as they could.

He wasn't sure what to do about it. He'd never had this happen before, or if it had, he'd ignored it—the same as he always ignored his gift. But if working with them could help Leah, he would.

"Is she there?" he asked, aware that Bram and Brandon were studying him.

The woman nodded. She held up her hands and showed eight fingers.

"There are eight humans in there?"

She nodded again. The male ghost moved to the side and pointed down a path.

"And we should go down that way?"

The two spirits nodded then faded away, looks of pain

on their faces. He didn't know what that meant, but he knew he owed them. He'd have to figure it all out later. Now, he needed to get to Leah.

Bram didn't ask him what the hell had just happened, but Brandon's look spoke volumes. Ryder wasn't sure he would be able to keep his secret much longer.

"She's in there," he said softly.

"You're going to explain this, brother," Brandon whispered. "Not now, because we need to get to Leah. But you will explain."

Ryder didn't answer but started down the path.

Bram merely mumbled something about secrets and powers and contacting Finn, but didn't say anything specific. Ryder didn't care at the moment. He just needed to find Leah.

They made their way down the path, and he almost growled as he saw the makeshift camp. The eight humans had set up large tents that smelled of weapons and chemicals. This must have been where they'd stored the bombs before they tried to take down the compound. There weren't any guards on this end, but he knew they might make a patrol this way at any moment. All eight of the humans were at the other end, and because it wasn't that large of a camp, he could see them all.

They surrounded a large wooden pole, and Leah stood strapped to it, her head down as if she were still drugged.

His claws ripped from his fingertips, but he held back the growl of agony that threatened to break free.

"They're going to burn her at the stake," Bram muttered. "Fucking barbarians. And they say wolves are the animals."

"We need to get her. Now." Ryder took a shallow breath. "If she's unconscious, she can't protect herself."

"That's probably one reason they used the damn drug in the first place," Brandon added. "That and getting her here so quietly. You saw Leah when she woke up in our medical bay. She fought back. She'd fight now if she could. Damn bastards."

Ryder let out a breath through his nose. "Bram, you go left, Brandon, you go right. I'll go down the damn center since they're not watching the tents. We get Leah out and find out whatever information we can about them from their uniforms or spare notebooks, and all of that. Then we get out of here. I don't trust this."

"Got it," Bram said. "We meet at the Talon den if we get separated? It's closer than the Redwoods."

"Deal."

The three prowled toward the camp in human form. He knew they'd shift if things went to shit, but he hoped they wouldn't have to. Ever since the Unveiling, they'd been careful not to become their wolves outside the den wards. They couldn't trust the human factions that wanted their deaths, nor could they trust the merely curious ones that got too close. There might be humans who thought the wolves should be left alone, but they weren't the ones in this camp. They weren't the ones with his mate tied to a damn pole about to be burnt at the stake.

"Luis said this one needed to die. That she would be an example for all witches," one of the humans said. "So we'll kill her now and live stream it so the others know not to fuck with Humans First. She's not human. She doesn't deserve to breathe our air." He let out a breath. "And when we're done here, we'll find that arrogant prick of a witch and kill him, too. We might be doing his bidding now because it's easy, but our doing anything he wants won't last."

Ryder held back a growl even though his wolf raged. He wanted to kill them all. That fucking Coven leader. Leah's father had orchestrated all of this. What the fuck? He shouldn't have been surprised, but hell. This was too much. And Ryder had heard of Humans First before. He knew it was a small group of humans who wanted everyone different to die. It seemed their propaganda was working because this was a lot more organized than it had been in the past. He'd tell Gideon all of this, of course, but first, he needed to get Leah down.

He couldn't risk them lighting the fire.

He could hear Bram in one tent, hopefully gaining any intelligence he could. Ryder knew the others couldn't hear it because they hadn't looked over. Bram was being damn quiet, but Ryder was wolf.

He hoped Brandon was on the other side, doing something similar. However, Ryder couldn't take on eight armed men at once and save Leah at the same time. Things were about to get tricky.

"Burn! Let the witch burn!"

Ryder let out a growl then. Low. Deadly. The humans turned to him, and he sprinted toward them. He was so fast that they hadn't had a chance to shoot at him before he had two of the men down. He didn't kill them, not with the live stream they'd spoken about going, but he did knock them out. Bram and Brandon came forward, knocking out a couple more before the guns began firing.

Ryder cursed as a bullet grazed his side. It burned, but he ignored it. He was about to hit another human when the man closest to Leah held up a match and grinned.

"Too fucking late, asshole!" He let the match fall, and the wood beneath Leah's feet caught flame. She remained unconscious, the ropes around her chest and waist keeping her upright though her head lolled.

Ryder did the only thing he could do and shifted. He tore through his clothes, his bones breaking, tendons snapping. He'd never shifted this fast in his life, and he didn't know why he could at that moment, but he'd take it. He knew he might have fucked over his family by becoming wolf on camera, but he didn't care. Not right then. He couldn't cut through the ropes without fangs and claws, and Leah needed him.

His body screamed in agony as he continued the shift even as he kept moving toward her. He'd never moved like this while shifting before and it only made the pain worse, but he pulled through it. As soon as he could, he leapt up on the burning pile and bit through the ropes, clawing at them at the same time. Bram and Brandon yelled from behind him and he trusted them to take care of the humans while he did this. As soon as Leah was free, she fell forward and he caught her on his back.

"Ryder?" she coughed, her voice sounding drugged.

Thank the goddess.

She wrapped her arms around his neck and climbed on top of him as much as she could. As soon as she was secured as much as possible, he leapt off the pile and landed on burnt paws. He growled but kept running with Leah on his back. He got as far as the trees before she fell off of him. He stopped and shifted back, just as painfully as before. As soon as he was able, he pulled her into his arms and kissed her temple.

"Ryder..."

"Leah..."

He didn't know what was going to happen next, but she was safe in his arms. That had to count for something. Because if it didn't...well...he wasn't sure what he'd do.

BRAM

"I cannot believe you let yourself get hurt like this, Bram. I thought you were faster than a couple of measly humans."

Bram winced as Charlotte stung not only his pride but also his side as she cleaned up his wound. She had gentle hands, but every time her skin brushed against his, he stiffened, unable to control himself. He hoped she just thought it was pain from the gash on his side and not the strike against his soul that it actually was.

"There were more than a couple," he grumbled. "And it's a lot harder to only slightly maim them with my strength, I'll have you know."

Charlotte let out a snort, but he saw the worry in her eyes. He reached out for her wrist without thinking. They both froze at the contact, but he didn't let go. He'd already reached out, so he may as well deal with the consequences.

"I'm okay, Charlotte," he said softly. His wolf nudged at

him, wanting more, but he ignored it. "We found Leah and got the information we needed. I'll heal."

Bram had never seen anything like it. Ryder had jumped through fire, literally, for the woman he claimed was not his mate. He might want to deny it, but Ryder would have to face the truth eventually. Bram knew how that felt far too well.

He'd known for too long that the woman in front of him was his. His wolf had wanted to claim her ever since they'd both been old enough to understand the full consequences and joy of mating. He knew her wolf wanted him, as well. And when he and Charlotte had fallen for each other and subsequently into bed to cement their bond, their worlds had shattered.

The bond never came, and now Bram was left alone and broken. He'd never known of a couple who'd gotten it wrong like they had. Perhaps it was just heavy attraction between them, but he wasn't sure that was the case. All he did know was that every day he and Charlotte remained as close as they were, they were only delaying the inevitable.

They weren't mates.

Or they were, but without a bond, which was just the same in the long run.

"Bram," she whispered.

He let her go before sighing. "I'm fine, Charlotte. Leave me alone for a bit, okay? I just need to think."

"Think about what?" she asked.

He met her gaze and pulled himself back from running a hand through her dark hair. "Just go."

She pressed her lips together then backed up before

turning away. He closed his eyes once she'd let the door close behind her. Damn it.

He wasn't enough for her. Something was missing, and he didn't know what, but there had to be an answer. And having them side by side in pain wasn't it.

I'm not enough, he repeated to himself.

He would never be enough.

As always.

CHAPTER
TEN

Leah closed her eyes, willing her body to stop shaking. She'd been back at home—Ryder's home —for almost half an hour now, and yet she couldn't make her body stop shaking like a damn leaf. She was safe. Ryder was safe. The rest of the Pack members were safe. The men who'd taken her were now in custody of the human police. Until the laws changed, she was still a citizen —witch or no—and the Humans First group had kidnapped her. The fact that Ryder and the others had been in control enough to let the human authorities take over, rather than doing what they wanted and taking out the price in the others' flesh, told her how much each step cost.

The drugs were out of her system thanks to the water they'd given her during the car ride back to the den. She'd been able to at least heal that part of her quickly. She still needed to work on the few cuts and abrasions on her skin, as well as the burns on her shins.

She shuddered a little more violently this time.

Goddess, she'd almost been burned at the stake. It was like the Middle Ages all over again. She'd heard horror stories growing up, as well as seen it done in movies, but she'd never thought in a million years that it would happen to her.

And yet, her people were dying from it because of the Humans First group. The authorities were doing their best, but in all reality, she knew she couldn't trust them fully. Not when the lines of the law were blurring for some. Just because the police had said they would take care of it, this time, didn't mean they would the next. It was up to each individual officer and detective, and with the way the world was changing, she wasn't sure she could put her faith in them.

Leah licked her lips and winced at the taste of smoke on them. She wasn't sure she'd ever look at a campfire or s'mores the same way again. If she hadn't been drugged, she would have probably been able to douse the fire and save herself, but her captors had rendered her unable. It killed her that she'd been so defenseless. She hadn't reacted quickly enough during the chaos of the bombings and that had cost her.

It could have cost her Ryder.

She cursed herself at the thought. He'd risked his life for her, and yet he still didn't want her as his mate. And the fact that she'd even thought that last part just told her how off she was. She shouldn't be worrying about mating and bonds while there were real issues at hand. Mating could take a back seat, along with her emotions.

First, she needed to stop shaking. Then she needed to make sure Ryder was okay. After that, she could deal with the fact that she hadn't been able to defend herself. Emotions could wait.

Forever if it were up to her.

As soon as they'd walked into Ryder's home—her safely in his arms—he set her on her bed. It didn't matter that he was hurt more than she was; he apparently had to carry her. She'd let him because she'd still been working the drugs out of her system, but now she was feeling much better and wanted to see if he was okay.

Gingerly, she pushed herself to her feet and let out a breath. It only hurt a little, and once she took a bath, she'd be back to her normal self. While it annoyed her that she couldn't heal others in the same fashion, at least her magic could keep her somewhat whole.

She padded down the hallway toward the living room where she could hear voices. Walker had his hands over the large burns on Ryder's side and stomach, his eyes closed and his mouth murmuring chants.

She put her hand over her mouth to hold back a gasp. She'd been so drugged out she hadn't seen the extent of Ryder's injuries. And since Walker was Healing them already, what she saw wasn't even the worst of it.

Ryder looked up as she entered but didn't say anything. Instead, he let his gaze trail down her body and back up again before settling on her eyes.

"You still have cuts and burns," he said finally, his voice a bit raspy.

"I'm going to have to Heal your throat, too, brother. You

have a bit of smoke inhalation." Walker shook his head but went back to work.

Leah had started toward the two of them before she thought better of it. She cupped Ryder's face with her hands since it was one of the only places where he didn't have cuts or burns.

"Never do that again, Ryder Brentwood. Your family almost lost you because you literally jumped through fire."

"You were going to die if I didn't," he growled, then let out a cough.

She pulled back before running her knuckles down his cheek. "You can't die for me, Ryder. You can't."

"I didn't die. Walker will Heal me, and we'll get you in the bath so you're healed, as well. Everything will be fine."

It wouldn't and she knew that. They were getting too close, letting emotions rule while they both knew they had to step back. They weren't going to cement the bond, and every day she stayed with him, it would only make it that much harder to walk away. And yet she couldn't leave. Not yet. She was torturing herself, but she couldn't help it.

"I'm going to be about twenty minutes more," Walker said casually. "Leah, do you mind getting us each a glass of water? I know we could use something stronger, but water should do."

Grateful for Walker's interruption, she gave him a nod then made her way back to the kitchen. She'd stopped shaking the moment she saw Ryder because then it wasn't about her. It was about the man who'd risked his life for her. He'd saved her, and she didn't know how to repay him. He and the Talons had saved her more than once now. She would be forever in their debt.

Roland would know what to do.

She stopped what she was doing and blinked. She hadn't thought of her twin in a few days, though she knew he'd been in the back of her mind no matter what. It hurt to think that he wouldn't be there to hear about what had happened. It hurt more that he wouldn't be able to take a stand against not only Humans First but the Coven, as well. He had always been better with words than her.

She'd told herself when she left his grave that she wouldn't allow Roland's death to rule her life. But it still ached that she didn't have him anymore. And now, Ryder had almost died, as well. It didn't matter how many times she told herself that they wouldn't be good for each other and that they would never mate; she knew if she'd lost him, she would have broken, shattered into a million pieces.

There was a reason the goddess had designed them to be optional mates, there would always be a connection because of it...until Ryder found another mate she supposed. But he'd told her he would never take a mate. However, no matter how hard she tried not to, she could only worry that maybe he'd meant that he would never take her as a mate. Maybe the next one would be the one that made him break his internal vow, the woman he'd want to bond with for eternity.

She didn't like thinking she wasn't good enough, but she couldn't help it.

She hadn't been good enough for the humans, hadn't

been good enough for the Coven. It was only fitting that she wasn't good enough to mate the Heir of the Talon Pack.

Leah might tell herself that she didn't want to mate with him because of the target she would put on his back, but now that she'd seen how the Pack worked, she knew differently. He would always be a target. For as long as there was the potential for war, he would always be in danger. Hell, he'd almost died for her, and they hadn't even mated.

It would be good for everyone if she left and never came back.

And yet, she knew she couldn't do that.

There had to be something wrong with her with the way she wanted him but he didn't want her, but she'd deal with that. And since she'd given her word to help the Pack, she would do that. She'd take it seriously and learn to protect herself and others. She had to work past the fear that had put Roland and her at risk in the cave and find a way to make the changes for herself. It was all she could do.

She was a witch; she had the power.

She'd prove it.

She carried all three glasses back without a tray and set them on the coffee table once she made it into the living room. She handed Ryder his and set a soft kiss on his lips. She'd needed to say her thanks and, frankly, needed to touch him. There was no going back from what had happened, no hiding from his family. Not with how he'd apparently reacted when he'd heard she was gone. Brandon had let a few things slip in the SUV, and Ryder hadn't been pleased. Yet she didn't care that Ryder hadn't wanted her to know he cared about her. Hadn't wanted her to know that he had been frantic with worry searching for her.

The sheer fact that he'd jumped on the burning pile to save her from the stake told her that much. The rest was just reassurance.

Instead of commenting on her rapid thoughts, she held out a glass to Walker. The Healer triplet took the glass and smiled. He nodded in thanks and chugged down the water quickly, sighing after he'd finished.

"Would you like some more? I know it takes a lot of energy to Heal. How about some food?"

Walker shook his head. "I'm almost done. I'll head home and get some protein before crashing. No need to worry about me, Leah. I've been at this for a long while. I can take care of myself."

From the strain in his eyes, she wasn't sure that was exactly the case. She couldn't get a bead on the Healer. One minute he was the laid-back triplet with a nice drawl, the next, he barked orders and hid secrets within his gaze. He wasn't the Brentwood she should be trying to figure out, however. That honor went to the other wolf in the room.

"If you change your mind, let me know. I don't want you passing out on the way to your house." She picked up her glass and took a deep drink, missing the taste. She'd already had three glasses since being saved, and yet, she couldn't get enough. Her magic was almost at full capacity—where she would do her best to keep it. She wouldn't be caught unawares again. She wasn't some helpless damsel, and she'd be damned if she acted like it once more.

She watched in silence as Walker finished his work.

She'd seen her own healing at work, of course, but seeing a true Healer help those in need was a thing of beauty. By the time Walker was through, she was ready for a long bath... and perhaps a bit more with Ryder. She knew she was an idiot to want him like she did, knowing there was no future for them, but not every intimate moment had to lead to mating and children. It could just lead to emotional healing.

Again, if she kept telling herself that, it would be true. It had to be.

When Walker left, she closed the door behind him and locked it. The keypad and hand scanner would allow him back in since Ryder had programmed his whole family with the right protocols, but they also had a mechanical lock in case the former became corrupted.

"You need to take a bath," Ryder said from behind her. She turned and let out a little sigh. She loved the way he looked without a shirt. She loved the way he looked period. Walker had Healed his wounds, but the new skin was still a tad pink. Plus, he still had dried blood on him that would need to be washed off.

"Bathe with me?"

His eyes glowed gold for a moment before he regained control of his wolf. "Let me shower while you start your soak. You already washed off the dirt and blood on your skin, but I haven't." He paused, and she held her breath. "Then I'll join you."

He held out a hand, and she took it as they made their way to his large bathroom in silence. His thumb brushed along her skin, and she leaned in to him when they reached the glory that was his bathroom. Seriously, she could have easily—and happily—lived in his bathroom alone.

"I can get the bath ready myself if you want to shower," she said, as he bent down over the taps.

He stood again and took her face in his hands. "Okay, little witch." He let out a shuddered breath. "I almost lost you, Leah."

She closed her eyes, took a deep breath, and then opened them again. When she leaned toward him and pressed her lips to his, he shook.

"Shower, Ryder. I'm okay. You're okay. We're alive. Remember that."

He kissed her a little harder then let her go. She had to take a few moments to compose herself so she didn't break down in tears, or worse, strip off his jeans herself and make love to him hard against the wall.

When she felt steady enough, she turned on the taps to as hot as they both could take it and added a few bath salts. While she normally liked her water pure and simple, both of them had been through a lot and a little bit of pampering couldn't hurt. Plus, she liked the scent of the salts. So much better than burnt wood and smoke.

The shower started behind her and she had to force herself not to turn around and look at Ryder through the clear glass door. She'd ogled him enough for the day. Leah quickly stripped out of her clothes, aware that Ryder was staring at her. She couldn't help but feel his intense gaze on her. It was almost palpable. She wasn't self-conscious about her body, especially with Ryder, so she slowly eased herself into the extra-large claw foot tub. The thing could easily fit three or four people, and it achieved the amazing feat of covering her knees and breasts at the same time. It was seriously her most favorite thing in the house.

As soon as she let the water lap over her skin, she let her magic ease through her pores. Her small cuts and burns healed quickly, the bruising taking a bit longer as they were deeper. Soon, she was healed, and the water was at a decent level. She reached up to turn it off, but Ryder beat her. She hadn't even heard the shower turn off since she'd been focusing on each bruise on her body.

"Lean forward," Ryder said. She did, bringing her knees to her chest so he would have space to maneuver around.

He slid into the tub right behind her, his legs encasing her on each side. He wrapped an arm around her waist and brought her back to his front. His rock-hard erection pressed into the small of her back, and she had to bite her lip to stop from moaning. She let her head rest on his shoulder and sighed, finally finding some semblance of peace for the first time since she'd felt that pinprick at her neck.

They lay there in silence, their breathing easing into soothing inhalations and exhalations in sync with one another. His hand gently ran up her stomach and to the space between her breasts before going back down again. It was an easy movement, one of comfort and familiarity. She had her fingers on his other arm, letting them dance softly along his skin so she could feel his touch, feel him.

"I almost lost you, too," she said finally, surprising herself. Ryder's hand stopped moving, his fingers right under her breast.

"Leah..."

"I know we're being careful, or at least trying, but I can't lie to myself anymore. I almost lost you because you were trying to save my life. I'll never be able to repay you for that...but I don't know what I would have done if you'd died." She was grateful he couldn't see her face.

"I don't know what I would have done if I had lost you either," he said after a moment of silence. "I just don't know."

"What are we doing, Ryder? How can it hurt this much yet feel so...right?"

He kissed the side of her neck, and she let out a sigh. When he buried his face there, she had to press her lips together before she said something monumentally stupid like she loved him or something.

"I can't form a bond with you, Leah. I...can't." His voice broke and he let out a growl. "You have no fucking idea how much I want to, damn it. I want you in my bed. In my life. I want you as my mate, but I can't."

She froze, her body suddenly cold. He'd never said that before, even if he'd hinted at it. If only he'd have enough trust in her to tell her why he couldn't. It broke her, even though she knew that she couldn't have him either. What would happen to him if she created the bond? What would the Coven do to him then?

"Maybe...maybe we could try without the bond?" She winced, prepared for his refusal. "We can do as we are...just without the bond."

He didn't speak for so long she was afraid she'd said

something wrong. Or maybe he was trying to find a way to let her down easily.

Instead, he slid his hand down her stomach to cup her sex. She gasped and rocked into him.

"We can try, Leah. We can damn well try. But if it hurts too much, if you need more, you need to let me know."

And he would let her go. He didn't say it, but she knew that's what he'd meant. They would have fun, have some sort of emotional tie and relationship, but they wouldn't bond. She could do that and hope that one day he would tell her why he couldn't bond with her. She deserved that much. But for now, she would take it.

"Okay," she whispered. Then he slid his fingers between her folds and rubbed her clit. She gasped, arching off his body. He wrapped his other arm around her and cupped her breast. His large, calloused fingers plucked at her nipple and she tilted her head toward him, needing his mouth.

He obliged, sliding his tongue along her lips so she would open for him. She sank into the kiss, rolling her hips as he fucked her with his fingers and played with her breasts. He teased along her entrance before sliding two fingers in, then sped up before slowing down to tease her once more. She gasped, aching, needing more, but he didn't stop his motions, didn't let her go over the edge. His cock dug into her back and she rubbed against it, wanting him to come along with her. He groaned and rocked his hips, as well. Water sloshed over the sides of the tub, but she didn't care. She just wanted him to take her to the top and let her fall in ecstasy. When he pinched her clit, she shook, her body bowing as she came hard against his hand. He didn't stop and she almost came again. Then he removed his hand and pushed her forward slightly so he could get out of the tub.

She felt cold at the loss of him but didn't have time to dwell on it. He had her out of the tub and in his arms in a blink. She moved so she could wrap her legs around his waist and rock into his cock again.

He groaned into her mouth and gripped her ass with his hands. When one finger played with her hole she stiffened, then leaned in to him as he slowly worked her, gentle and yet heated.

"I'm going to fuck you there one day, little witch. Do you like the sound of that?"

She nodded and kissed him again, loving the way he growled and wanted more of her. When he sat her down on the edge of the counter and leaned in front of her, she gasped.

He spread her legs wide and licked his lips. "Keep your legs open. Can you do that? Can you keep your legs steady when I lick your pretty cunt?"

She bit her lip and moaned. "I can try."

"I'd say there is no try, only do, but that might break the mood." He slid his finger up and down her slit even as she gasped a laugh.

"We need to watch that movie," she said as he slid one finger into her, curling up so he rubbed along that bundle of nerves that made her eyes cross.

"Later. First I need my feast." Then he leaned forward and lapped at her, eating her until she could barely breathe. His beard brushed along her inner thighs and lower lips until she couldn't formulate words. He fucked her with two fingers, then three, even as he kept his mouth on her, sending her quickly over the edge once more.

Even as she called out his name and clenched around his fingers, he kept moving. He stood up, grabbed a condom from the drawer, and slid it over his length. Ryder gripped her hips, and she held onto the edge of the counter so she could slide off.

"Fuck me, Ryder."

"I can do that, little witch. I'll fuck you until we're both breathless and sated. Just make sure you fuck me just as hard."

"I can do that. Just get inside me. Now."

He grinned at her, tightened his hold on her hips, and thrust into her hard. In one stroke, he filled her so full she could barely breathe. She wrapped one leg around his waist and slid the other up his body so it rested over his shoulder. He held onto that ankle, kissing and licking her calf and behind her knee as he fucked her hard on the counter. She gripped the edge until her knuckles went white, rocking her hips ever so slightly and tightening her pussy so she squeezed his cock. He must have liked that because his eyes glowed brighter and he picked up the pace.

When he lifted her other leg to his shoulder and gripped her ass, she let out a yelp, reaching for his shoulders to hold on. He held her weight with ease, lifting her and positioning her so he went deeper than he ever had before. Their gazes met and she held her breath, unable to think, to speak, to do anything but feel.

He pulled her up and slammed her down on his cock,

the sensation so fucking good she almost passed out right then, unable to even come because she knew if she did, she'd shatter. But he seemed to know where her mind had gone and slid home again, this time holding her down over him. She came then, knowing it was too much and not caring. He came as well, filling the condom, the sensation so warm and so him. She wanted him bare within her, wanted to feel him pump into her and fill her full. But she knew that wouldn't happen.

It would never happen. Because if it did, they'd create the bond. Instead, she would have to deal with a condom for however long they made this work.

It would have to be enough, though. Because she wasn't sure what she would do without him. And frankly, she was afraid of what he'd do without her. They'd have to live with the decisions they'd made and learn to deal with this new form of...whatever this was.

But with the feel of Ryder deep within her and the sated state of her body and emotions at that point, she didn't seem to care.

She would take Ryder Brentwood however she could. Because there wasn't another option. Only pain and yearning. Until they broke. Again.

CHAPTER
ELEVEN

Ryder stared at the man who had caused so much pain, so much fear, and resisted the urge to kill him where he stood. Slowly. Or perhaps not too slowly, as Ryder would rather be back at his den with the woman who made his heart stop—even if he didn't know what the hell he was going to do with her.

Luis, the Coven leader, a water witch with no qualms about killing, and the father of Leah, sat before him in his ornate, wooden, long-backed chair that looked more like a throne than an assembly chair. His peers surrounded him; the same witches who'd run toward the back exit when the first bomb blew. Only a few of those who remained had come to Ryder's side during the blast. Those would be the witches the wolves would negotiate with and work with to help their people in the future.

The Alphas had agreed, and now Finn and Ryder would do what must be done to take the next step. Their worlds were burning, literally. According to their contacts in Washington, the government would be revealing their plan and laws soon. Once that happened, the current standstill would end, and they'd have to face whatever came. Ryder wasn't looking forward to that in the least. But that hadn't happened yet, and first, he needed to get a few things straight.

The witches in front of him were one of those pieces.

Leah stood by Ryder's side, healed and angry. Or maybe he was the one who was angry. Leah looked more...resigned about the fact that her father had tried to kill her. As if that had been the inevitable conclusion to the relationship that had never been. He wanted to wrap his arm around her shoulders and bring her close, but he wasn't sure she would accept it.

Something had changed between them, and he couldn't figure out what it was exactly. But this wasn't the time to worry about what his wolf ached for or how the woman beside him made him feel. He had to take care of the problem at hand, then he could worry about himself.

That was how he'd functioned in the past, and that was how he would have to now—even if it hurt like hell.

"You've summoned us here for a reason, wolf," Luis snapped. "Get on with it. We don't have all day to deal with your people. We have a war of our own to deal with."

Ryder tilted his head and studied the man in front of him. Sweat slicked the witch's forehead and his hands were clenched in front of him. Luis knew something was up and was damn worried about it.

Good.

"We're here to deal with that war, or have you forgotten?" Ryder asked calmly. Leah put her hand on his back, settling the wolf beneath his skin that wasn't so calm. "We're also here so you can see that our people, all our people, are alive after the attack."

Luis raised his chin. "And?"

"Why did you do it?" Ryder asked, his voice low. "Why did you sacrifice your daughter and risk the lives of your people to help the humans who want us all dead? It doesn't help anything except to perpetuate the violence."

Gasps sounded in the room, but Luis merely narrowed his eyes. "You dare accuse me of this? What proof do you have?"

Finn growled beside Ryder and pressed a button on his phone. The voice of the human who had called out Luis's name at the camp sounded as he told of his plans and the connection to Luis. They hadn't recorded it when they'd been preparing to fight but had gotten his confession again before the cops came. At least, Finn had, once he'd made it to the camp. Ryder had only been thinking about Leah—something that was dangerous. But with the mating urge riding him hard, he couldn't function like he needed to.

"Lies!" Luis screamed and stood. "You want the witches dead, that is why you come in here with your false accusations. Get out of here before I show you what kind of witch I am. What power I wield."

"Oh, I think we already know what kind of witch you are," Leah said smoothly. "You're the kind of witch who cheats on his wife and lies to the woman who fathered twins for you. You're the kind of witch who spends years,

years, hunting them down and trying to snuff out their lives so the world doesn't look down on you. You're the kind of witch who makes contact with organizations who not only hate the paranormal but want to use them for their means so you can kill two witches who truly mean nothing to you. You're the kind of witch who, after having one twin killed, will find every way possible to have your daughter's life ended. Even start a war with the wolves in order to get it done. You're no true witch. You're a traitor in every way possible."

Ryder wanted to throw his head back and howl at her words. She didn't sound broken or defeated. She sounded strong. She sounded wolf.

Leah raised her chin, her hands at her sides. "You killed Roland. I know you had something to do with my mother's death. And now you've risked the lives of your people, the lives of the wolves who wanted to help the witches in the Unveiling. All so you can end my life."

"You heard the evidence," a female witch told Luis. "We all heard it. I don't know about every word this young woman is saying, but I know the way you work, Luis. Why would you do this? Why would you cooperate with the enemy?"

Luis stood tall, his eyes dark, spittle forming at the corner of his mouth as he shouted. "This piece of trash shouldn't be here. She has no right to be in our proceedings. I did what I had to in order to protect our line, our people."

Ryder's claws slid from his fingertips, his body shaking with rage. "You almost killed my Pack. That makes you an enemy of the Talons."

"And the Redwoods," Finn added.

"You're nothing. Just a bunch of ill-bred dogs. You're the reason we're forced to come out of hiding to begin with." Luis opened his arms and pushed them forward. Magic shot toward them, a wall of water that didn't seem to touch the witches came out of nowhere.

Ryder turned to protect Leah, but should have known better. She slid her arms up, a wall of water of her own forming from the glasses of water on the tables and the small pool on the other side of the open door. He hadn't noticed it before, but his Leah had.

Leah's magic pulsated as she clenched her jaw. Luis's water slammed into Leah's before spreading out as if it were a wave smashing into the rocks. The water drenched the witches nearest to the wolves, forcing screams from them.

"Stop what you're doing, Luis!" One of the witches called out. "You're through. You risked all of us for your own vendetta."

Luis held one hand out toward that witch and sent a spiral of water over the man's body. The other man screamed, trying to use his own magic, but Luis was too strong.

However, he wasn't as strong as Leah.

Every single witch began to use their magic, throwing fire, earth, water, and gusts of wind toward each other. Their own civil war erupting in front of them.

Ryder turned toward the spirits in the room, his body stiff from holding back. He wanted to shred Luis's face but refrained because it was not his duty. Leah needed to fight, needed to stand up and be the warrior she was. It didn't help his wolf, though. The spirits floated right below the celling, pain and rage evident on their faces.

Leah was the only witch protecting the wolves, as the other witches were too worried about themselves and their own battles. While the wolves would be able to care for themselves, he knew something else had to happen in order for them to truly win.

"Help," he whispered toward the spirits closest to them. The spirits looked sharply at him, surprise showing on their features.

He'd only asked for help once from them and that was for Leah. Now he did it again for her and would keep doing so. He lied to himself daily when he said it would be easy to walk away from her. He lied to himself when he'd said he didn't want her as a mate. He loved her, damn it. Loved the way she fought for herself, loved the way she tried to hold herself back because he was the fucking idiot hurting them both.

And yet, he knew he'd have to keep doing it.

Because of things like this.

The spirits came toward him, slashing at his skin, pulling energy from his wolf in a way he hadn't thought possible. He went to his knees, his body shaking.

The others around him came to his side, Finn at his back as he tried to fight off what he couldn't see.

Only Ryder could see them.

Only Ryder could hear them.

Only Ryder could feel them.

Only Ryder...

He didn't know what was going on. He'd never used the

sprits like this, had never had them use him. Each spirit touched him and then went back to where Luis stood, forming a circle around him.

Ryder took a deep breath and looked toward Leah. She had her arms up, protecting the Pack, but her eyes were wide. She kept her attention split between him and what was in front of her, and he knew she'd get hurt if she kept doing it.

"I'm fine!" he called out over the rush of screams and magic. "Keep up the wall."

She didn't look like she believed him, but turned away, her attention fully on her magic once again.

Ryder stood on shaking legs, refusing to look weak. The wolves around him were on edge, wanting to fight an enemy they couldn't see. The witches were focused on hurting one another, a war amongst themselves brewing.

The spirits that had taken some of his energy continued to swirl around Luis and his wife Darynda before finally attacking. The couple screamed as they fell to their knees, the unseen enemy doing their jobs. He wasn't sure why the spirits were doing this, why they were helping, but they were.

He hadn't known he could ask for help like this, and he knew damn well the cost had been his energy. He hoped nothing more. He wasn't the one controlling them, and he knew only a spirit witch had the ability to even try that. But he had asked, and they had helped.

You'll pay for that, useless pup.

His uncle shouted in his ear, and his wolf growled. Ryder ignored it; instead, coming to Leah's side. The witches in front of him were either down for the count or fighting their final battles of the day. Smoke wafted in the room, and puddles of water dotted the floor and mixed with earth to make mud that spoke of magic and death.

"You can stop, baby," he whispered, wrapping his arms around Leah's waist. "You saved us."

Leah let her hands fall, and the wall of water slid to the ground, leaving waves until it finally settled into a pool. Finn came to Leah's other side and the rest of the wolves guarded their backs.

"I...what happened?" she asked, a frown on her face.

Ryder let out a breath. He knew she wasn't talking about the magic that occurred, but rather what had happened to him. He really wasn't ready to talk about it yet, but he knew he'd run out of time.

"Let's go home first," he said softly.

"You'll have to explain it to all of us at some point," Finn challenged.

Ryder let out a small growl but didn't counter. "Let's get home." He turned toward the mayhem in front of them. "When you get your act together and find yourselves ready to discuss the future, contact us."

The female witch that had condemned Luis earlier— the pregnant one who had tried to help during the attack— nodded. "We have a few things to clean up." She gestured toward Luis's and Dayrnda's prone bodies on the floor. "Thank you for understanding."

He squeezed Leah to his side. Her father had died, not by Ryder's hand, but by his command. She might not know it yet, but he would have to tell her soon. He'd have to tell all of them soon. Secrets only led to pain and death. He'd known that as a child, and yet hadn't told them of his gift until he'd almost lost Leah.

Now he'd have to face the consequences.

As well as the woman he knew he'd have to leave for good. Because his so-called gift had just killed her father and hurt Ryder in the process. There was no way he could allow Leah to be hurt from it...even if walking away killed him every moment in the process.

―――――

LEAH STOOD by the partially frozen lake and breathed out, the air so cold she could see her breath. Her body ached from the use of her magic, and her heart ached from the lack of use when it came to feeling.

No, that wasn't quite right.

Maybe she used her heart too much.

Her father was dead. As was the woman he'd married. She officially had no blood relations left in the world. She was alone, far more alone than she'd thought she was when Roland had died.

Yet it wasn't because the man who had hated her more than he'd loved his Coven was dead. It was because the man she loved, the man the goddess had blessed her with held back. He not only held back his emotions, his feelings for her, but he also held back his secrets.

She had a feeling that the reason he held back, the reason he refused to mate with her, had to do with whatever the hell had happened in that Coven meeting. Ryder had done something. He'd been in pain, she'd seen the agony on his face, and yet he wouldn't tell her why.

Luis and Darynda were dead, but she didn't know how it had happened. The witches thought one of them had done it, a stray spark of fire or water or earth. But it hadn't been, the wolves knew that.

Ryder had done something to end the lives of those who had not only threatened and hurt her but had endangered the entire Pack.

He would have to come clean soon, she knew, but he hadn't done so yet. It had only been a few hours since the incident, but he'd remained quiet about it.

And she hated it. She was so...angry. She deserved far better than a man who hid himself from her, especially if it hurt them both. She held fault, as well. She'd stayed away to keep him safe, and yet he'd almost been hurt anyway. The man who had tried to kill her for so many years was gone, as was that particular threat to Ryder's life.

She'd fought to keep alive for so long, and now she would fight for something more.

For Ryder.

But first, he'd have to tell her his secrets. Because it hurt that he didn't trust her enough to reveal them.

She was on Pack land, a stranger who had brought trouble to their door. Yet they hadn't pushed her away. Neither had Ryder for that matter, though he'd still kept his distance. Maybe one day Gideon would bring her into the Pack as a member, even if she weren't mated to Ryder. Could she do that? Could she be part of a Pack where she would be forced to see the one man she loved every day and not be able to mate with him? They may have told each other they would try to be with one another without the bond, but as time moved on, she wasn't sure she could do that.

She was better than that. Worth more than that.

And that was the crux of it, wasn't it?

She'd finally found her worth. She'd protected the Pack and saved them all. And now she had to save herself.

A cold wind slid over her skin and she shivered. She'd come to the lake because her body needed the water, even if it were frozen over in most places. With just her touch, she could melt the ice and have herself a nice warm bath.

Determined to wash away some of the day, she stripped to her skin and sent out a pulse of magic. The edge of the lake closest to her began to melt, the crack of ice loud in the silence, echoing off the large trees. The Talon land would make any witch proud. Easy access to earth and water with an immense history of caring for the territory and land. While many of the forests around the country had been pilfered, the goddess had aided the wolves with their dens, and within those dens, the land reflected its true nature and connection to the earth and to the moon goddess.

The Talon land called to her, much like Ryder did.

She only hoped that both wouldn't scar her for life.

The man would push her away while the land might reject her. Everything else had in the past, and she wouldn't put it past the moon goddess to reject her claim, or rather, her need, of the Talon land.

Leah dipped one foot into the lake and sighed. While the rest of the lake either had ice over it or had a slushy look to it, her magic had created an almost hot spring where it had pulsed. She moaned deeply as she submerged herself into the water up to her neck. The lake called to her magic and she let it soak into her skin. Normally, she wouldn't waste her magic on making her own hot tub within a natural lake, but the water would replenish her quickly. And frankly, she needed time to think. Time to heal.

Her magic tingled along her skin, the water soothing her soul yet not her anger.

When she sensed rather than saw Ryder approach, she kept her eyes closed and her back to him. The sound of clothes rustling reached her ears and she dunked her head under the water, needing the moment to clear her thoughts.

As she stood, breathing in fresh air and sliding her hands through her hair, Ryder's arms went around her waist. She didn't stiffen, but neither did she lean into his hold like she wanted to.

The anger beneath the surface didn't burst through, but it was there. Waiting.

"You look beautiful in the moonlight," Ryder said softly, his breath warm on her neck. "That sounds like a line. I'm sorry. What I mean is, you look like a goddess in your own right. Add the magic you used to create your own winter oasis...you stun me. You are so powerful, Leah. Brilliance beneath a soft surface. I...you take my breath away."

She pressed her lips together then turned in his arms. When she opened her eyes, she let out a breath. He stared down at her, his eyes intense. It wasn't his wolf there with her, but the man. The man wanted her, and the man had said the words that, at any other moment, would make her fall for him once more.

She wanted to tell him that she loved him, wanted to ask him if he was okay from the attack before. She had so much she wanted to tell him, but instead of any of that, she let the anger come through...the anger and the hurt.

"Why don't you trust me?"

It came out like a growl, but it was a plea, not a whisper.

Ryder's eyes widened ever so slightly, and she saw the shame slide through them. "I trust you, Leah. I trust you more than anyone else in my life."

"That's a fucking lie." He stiffened at her curse. Probably because she didn't use those words as much as him, or at least she hadn't yet. He was in for a new version of her. "You don't trust me enough to tell me why you won't mate with me. You're denying me a future with you. You're denying me children, you're denying me love and a mating bond. And you keep telling me it's for a reason, but you won't tell me that reason. That's not trust."

"I'll tell you, Leah. I'll tell you everything."

That should have warmed her, but it might be too late.

"Why now? Because you're in a corner? Because that still doesn't speak trust."

He cupped her face with one hand and slid the other through her wet hair. "I'll tell you everything, Leah. I promise. I didn't tell you before because I was ashamed." He closed his eyes. "I'm broken, Leah. So fucking broken that I'll break you, too."

She let out a little sob, tears filling her eyes. "I'm already broken, Ryder. Mates are supposed to put each other back together." Anger filtered through her again, but sorrow slid in right behind it, taking over.

Her heart broke once more, knowing that while Ryder might tell her everything, it didn't mean he'd create the bond. He'd said he was protecting her, but when would he get it in his head that she could protect herself?

Instead of saying anything else, she rested her cheek on his chest and let his heartbeat calm her. Steam drifted off the ice blocks as the water around them remained heated from her magic. They stood naked and embracing within the frozen lake, the picture a symbol of where she was—frozen within who she was meant to be and who Ryder thought she could be.

PATIENCE

Charles McMaster replayed the stream on the screen in front of him. He'd seen wolves change before, of course. He had his subjects in the lab that he'd seen change from human to wolf and back again countless times. There was something so...cathartic about seeing a man break in half and become a beast.

The world had also seen shifters change before during the Unveiling. There was nothing new about this, except for the fact that they'd been with humans when they did it. They'd protected the witch tied to the burning pyre. And now, it seemed that part of the human population was slowly moving to the wolf side of the debate.

Save one damsel in distress, and suddenly, women swooned for the blue-eyed wolf.

McMaster wasn't interested in the wolf on the screen for that, however. Something told him this particular wolf was important. And he'd learned long ago to trust those gut instincts. He wanted this wolf for his own. He had a few wolves in his possession, but it wasn't enough.

This wolf needed to be his.

According to his notes, this wolf was the Heir of the Talon Pack. The Heir apparently held some worth. McMaster wanted that for himself. He'd already set forth plans to ensure this Heir would be his. The wolves wouldn't know what hit them.

He turned off the screen and rolled his shoulders before locking up his secret office and heading toward the medical rooms. He wanted to check on his specimens in the cages. As usual, they screamed, the toxic sludge in their veins probably killing them at this point. They would die for science, for power, and they would have to cling to a world of no hope...except for the hope for him, of course.

McMaster, like his accomplice General Montag, wanted the wolves locked in their dens like the animals they were. While Montag wanted the shifter's powers for his own purposes, McMaster wanted the beasts put to death.

He'd use them for his own power, then he'd have them die by their own fate. He had a bill coming that he would pay dearly for. But that bill would force the wolves to be outed completely in society, and therefore, be caged like the animals they were within their dens. It would make them easier to study, and eventually end.

Easier for slaughter.

Easier for planning.

Easier for him.

CHAPTER
TWELVE

Ryder cupped Leah's shoulder as she dried her hair with a towel. The soft fabric slid along his wrist, and she shook her head, pulling the towel away from her hair. Her long, honey-brown hair spilled down her back and over his arm. After leaving the icy lake and putting on their dry clothes over cold and wet bodies, they'd made it back to his place. Throughout that and their shower, they'd kept their hands on each other as if they couldn't keep a distance beyond the one he'd made already. They'd also remained silent.

When they'd passed other Packmates on the way to the house, they'd nodded at them, but that was it.

They'd said enough in the lake to know if they were to break their silence too soon, they might break everything else.

He'd hurt her. Hurt her enough that she thought it was her fault. And that was something that could not be allowed. No matter what he did, no matter how he messed up, it wasn't Leah's fault. He was the one with the shattered gift and a wolf who tore him up when he shifted. While he hadn't wanted to force his pain on her, he'd hurt her just the same.

"You're thinking so hard I can almost hear your thoughts," Leah said softly. She turned in his arms and rested her forehead on his chest. "I'm not weak, Ryder. You can lean on me too, you know. You don't have to do everything on your own."

He cupped her face, forcing her gaze to his. "I've never once thought you were weak. From the moment you woke up and fought to protect yourself from the unknown, I knew you were stronger than anyone I had ever met."

She blew out a breath. "You say that, yet you don't treat me as if you believe it."

His thumb ran along her cheekbone, and she ever so slightly leaned in to his hold. "You can take care of yourself, and yet, sometimes, I don't want you to have to. That's not only my wolf in action, but the man."

Leah pulled away from his hold but took his hand. "Let's go to the living room and sit down. Then you can tell me what you need to."

Ryder was the Heir of the Talon Pack. He had fought for his Pack and protected his own. He'd withheld his secrets so enemies could not use them, as well as to keep his shame from those who loved him.

And now he would have to face the consequences of his decisions. Because he'd been blessed by the goddess with a potential mate, and yet he'd pushed her away while still keeping a small hold on her. He didn't deserve her, yet he didn't want to let her go.

They made their way to the living room and sat next to one another on the couch. Leah sank into the cushions but didn't look as relaxed as she was trying to portray. He'd been the one to do that. She may have lost her father that morning, but the pain on her face wasn't born of that.

"I wasn't born the Heir," he said after a few moments of silence. Leah didn't respond except to grip his hand. "My uncles and father were the ones who held the mantles of power from the goddess. You know some of my history, my family's history. But in order for you to understand why... just why...I'll tell you more."

She squeezed his hand. "Just say what you need to, how you need to. I told you about my family and the Coven. So I understand. Sometimes, you have to go the long way."

He kissed her knuckles then rubbed his thumb along them. "My father was a sadist. While that, in itself, wouldn't normally be a horrific thing, he held the power of the Pack and not only liked to deliver pain, he liked to deliver humiliation, torture, and death. He beat Gideon until my brother, my Alpha, couldn't walk. He...he hurt Brynn to the point I didn't think she'd be whole again."

He let out a shaky breath. "Each uncle verbally and physically abused us. Mitchell and Max's father saved his pain only for his sons, and I don't know the details. It's not my place to know them unless they are ready to reveal. We grew up in pain and fire. So much distrust and agony came from the men before us, the goddess began to disown us."

Leah met his gaze, and he took a deep breath.

"Until Gina from the Redwood Pack and Quinn mated, there hadn't been a mating in the Talon Pack for fifteen years." He closed his eyes. "Those fifteen years were a time of rebuilding. Gideon killed our father because of his crimes, and most of the other uncles lost their battles during the Redwood and Central war."

Leah squeezed his hand once more. "I know most of the history of the war, Ryder. I know the atrocities of the Centrals. As well as your uncles."

"You don't know all of them," he said softly. "As I said before, I was not born the Heir. But as the second son of the Alpha, I knew one day I would become the Heir. That is how things are supposed to work. Once the next generation awakens and grows into their wolves, they become the new powers. The older ones step down as they train their counterparts. That is how the Redwoods are doing it now, and that was how the Talons should have done it. And yet we didn't. Our uncles refused to train us. They refused to allow their wolves to give up any of their powers in the hierarchy. It broke our Pack. Almost completely."

Ryder pushed back the memories of the screams, the pain, the disappearances of those close to him. Each of their uncles had mated at one point in their lives, yet each of the women had died at the hands of the Brentwood family.

"For a long time, I didn't believe the Talons deserved the goddess's forgiveness."

"Ryder."

"I know that was wrong. The innocent deserved far more than forgiveness. But I'm going off track." He let out a slow breath. "Uncle Timothy was the Heir before me. He was the one uncle most of the family believed held a nicer side. It was a lie. Is a lie."

"What do you mean?"

"Timothy allowed the Pack to believe he was the one on their side. He never showed his cruelty because he wanted to be the one they relied on, all the while undercutting them. He only showed his true self to one person." He paused. "Me."

"Oh, Ryder." She climbed into his lap, and he tucked her under his chin, needing her touch. His wolf pushed at him, wanting her even closer.

"He beat me until I was sure I wouldn't be able to shift and heal. Our Healer, my other uncle, had to have known I was in pain. The rest of the family who had powers had to have felt it along the bonds, but they did nothing. I almost died at least a dozen times. And each time he'd force me to shift. Because of that, I think, shifting is so painful that I hate doing it."

His wolf whimpered and he wanted to curse.

"I don't hate my wolf. He's...he's the other part of my soul. But letting him out is agony."

Leah nuzzled into him, calming not only his wolf, but the rest of him, as well. "Tell me everything, Ryder. I know that's not all. You hate yourself and push me away because of something. It can't be your wolf alone."

He kissed the top of her head. "You're right. That's part of my past, but not all of it." He took a deep breath. "I was beaten, forced to turn when I shouldn't have, and had to hide it all for fear Timothy would kill Brynn. Yet through it all, everything was made worse because I have a...a gift."

Leah pulled away. "Does it have to do with how you found me in the woods? Or what happened to Luis and Darynda?"

Goddess, she was so smart, so strong. He didn't deserve her.

"I can see spirits," he blurted.

Holy hell. He'd never said that before. Never revealed his deepest, darkest secret. And yet, Leah was the only one he could ever envision telling. Maybe when he told the others later it would be easier, but telling Leah...that was everything.

He cleared his throat. "I see the dead, can hear them, feel them sometimes."

"Oh, Ryder. That...gift. No wonder you're so silent sometimes. The voices of the dead can be overwhelming. I'm not a spirit witch, but I know of the powers."

She understood. Just like that, she understood.

"For the first half of my life, they screamed at me. They never asked me for anything, but they shouted and tried to get their hooks into my wolf. I wasn't strong enough to get them to stop, but I was strong enough to keep my wolf and my soul. Now they ask for things or scream. They brush by me, taking a little bit out of me with each sighting. Only recently have I tried to...not control, but use my gift." And both times were for her.

"You needed someone to guide you, Ryder. I know if you had been in another Pack, an elder would have helped. Or even an earth or water witch."

"What do you mean a water witch?"

Leah pulled away from him slightly so she could look at

his face. "Ryder, water witches commune with the spirits. We cannot hear them unless it's on the slight mist of a wave newly born, but we can feel their presence. We're the most sensitive of the witches when it comes to those who have been lost to us. We cannot control or send them through the Veil as spirit witches can, but we can aid."

"I...I didn't know that." It didn't make sense. How could he not know that? It changed everything...but he couldn't hope. Not when he'd spent a century giving up on the idea of a future with a mate.

He'd pushed Leah away to protect her, and yet... had it been for nothing?

"Oh, my Ryder." She cupped his face. "Don't you see? The goddess knew what she was doing when she brought us together. You're in so much pain, my wolf. I want to help you. I need to. You should have been trained in your gift, and I could rightly kick their fucking asses for daring to leave you alone as you are. You need to tell your family, darling. They need to know who you are, what you are. I'm honored you told me, and I will cherish your secret. But Ryder, you are more than your gift, more than your wolf, more than your loyalty. You are more than who you think you are."

"If I were to tell them, then I'd risk the spirits coming after them...or risk Timothy."

Her eyes widened. "Your uncle is still here? He didn't cross the Veil?"

His uncle screamed in his ears even as some of the other spirits cried for what they'd lost in their lives. It was always a dull throb in the back of his mind, but since he'd spoken of it, it only got louder. What would he do if Leah could help him? Could he risk her? Or was that even a risk? He just didn't know.

"He haunts me every hour. I don't see him like I see the others, but I can hear him."

"And he makes you feel like shit because he's a fucking asshole." Leah pressed her lips together and inhaled through her nose. "Ryder. You do not have to do this alone."

"I pushed you away because I couldn't have you."

"You wouldn't," she counted.

"Couldn't. No. I couldn't, Leah. A mating bond can force the other person to deal with the wolf's gifts and powers. Not only would you have to deal with the excess bonds of a healing and growing Pack as the mate of the Heir, but you might also end up with my abilities."

Leah stood, her hands fisting. "And you don't think I can handle that? You didn't give me a choice. How do you think that makes me feel? You say I'm strong and you let me protect your family with my magic, but you undercut all of that by saying you can't mate with me."

He stood and cupped her face, his wolf howling within. "I couldn't see you die because of it. Don't you understand? Every time I use a spirit, every time it slides through me, I weaken. I couldn't let that happen to you. I don't know what will happen when a bond forms. What if it gets worse? What if it kills you? I see death, little witch. What if death takes a new form with a mating bond? I've heard of gifts mutating before. I didn't want to risk you."

Leah let out a little growl. If he hadn't been so sure the

growl was because he'd hurt her, he'd have thought it was damn sexy.

"You don't get to decide that, Ryder. But, but, I will forgive you. Only because life is hell and you had to live over a century burning in its flames. You didn't know what to do with your gift, you weren't trained. You didn't know that as a water witch, I could help you maintain your control and find your peace. So I will forgive you. But you don't get to keep secrets from me anymore. You can't. When we decided to try to be together without the bond, I tried to understand. But now that I know why you pushed me away, I don't know if I can be with you without the bond."

He kissed her softly, his wolf scraping at him. "I want you, Leah. I want you in my life, in my bed. The goddess showed me what we could have, and I pushed it away because I didn't understand. I didn't know. Forgive me, Leah. Forgive me for risking everything because I thought I knew better."

He was a dominant wolf and not good at groveling. He just prayed that what he'd done would be enough.

She kissed his jaw then ran her hands down his chest. "I'm your mate, Ryder. I'm not going away. With you I found out how to be the witch I needed to be. You made me safe, my wolf. You found me during the darkest part of my life and brought me to the light. Trust me and what the goddess gives us."

"Be my mate, Leah. Be with me." She nodded as he pressed his lips to hers, his wolf howling.

He didn't know what would come next, what would happen once they mated, but he knew he couldn't push her away any longer. The mating urge rode him hard, and frankly, he knew if he had to face a war with the humans and whatever battles happened with his Pack, he wanted Leah by his side...and in his heart.

She'd told him she could handle it, and he would have to trust the goddess. He'd never had that kind of faith before, but maybe, just maybe, it would work out.

Leah's hand gripped him through his sweats and he groaned. "Get out of your head and get inside me, Ryder. I need you."

He let out a deep chuckle then gripped her ass, grinding himself to her. "I can do that, little witch. I can fill you up and make you come so hard we'll both be passed out, sated."

"That's a lot of talk, but not a lot of action." She licked her lips then went to her knees. "Maybe I should show you just exactly what I'm talking about." With that, she pulled him out of his sweats and pumped him hard.

He groaned, tangling his fingers in her hair. "Have I told you I love your mouth? You know exactly what to do with your tongue. I could fuck your mouth all day."

She hummed along his length and rolled his balls in her palm. He let his head fall back as he slowly worked in and out of her mouth. She savored him as if she couldn't get enough. When his balls tightened, he pulled out then lifted her up into his arms.

"I wasn't done," she said on a laugh as he stripped her down to her skin.

"I don't want to come in your mouth first. I want to fill up that beautiful pink cunt of yours and mate. Does that sound like a plan? You ready for my cock in your pussy, little witch?"

He smacked her ass as she went silent, as if she were thinking. When she moaned, he smacked it again, rubbing the sting as her legs melted underneath her, even in his arms. She kissed his chin and he lowered his face, taking her mouth. They kissed softly, slowing increasing the fervor as their passion ignited. Together, they laid on the carpet, the thickness soft and sensual against their skin.

He kissed up and down her body, licking at her nipples, suckling as she moaned underneath him. When he parted her thighs to check her readiness, he let out a growl of his own.

"You're so wet for me, little witch. Did you like my cock in your mouth? Did that turn you on?"

"I loved your cock in my mouth," she teased. "But I'm going to love to have your cock in my cunt even more."

He growled at her dirty words and moved so he hovered over her, his cock at her entrance. "Do you know what comes next?" She winked at him, and he laughed. He never thought to mate with another, and he damn sure didn't think he'd laugh and have fun with his mate during their mating bond. Leah was perfect for him, and he'd kick himself until the end of days for taking so long. "I meant the mating, little witch."

She nodded and arched up against him, her nipples pressing into his chest. "Yes. You'll fill me and come, connecting our human halves. Then you'll bite my shoulder, marking me as yours for all to see and mating your wolf to my witch."

He kissed her softly. "Perfect, darling."

"Can I bite you, too?" She sounded almost shy.

He growled again and reached down to hold the base of his cock so he wouldn't come at her words. "You can bite me all you want. I will proudly wear your mark."

She licked her lips and met his gaze. As she sucked in a breath, he slowly, oh so slowly, entered her. His hands roamed her breasts and arms as hers did the same to his back. He worked in and out of her, loving the way her pussy clenched around him when he reached a certain spot. Their tongues tangled as they kissed, their bodies sweat-slick as they made love.

When his fangs elongated, Leah tilted her head, baring her neck for him. His wolf howled as he slowly bit into the meaty part of her shoulder where it met her neck. He'd heard from others that it wasn't a painful bite, but he was still as gentle as he could possibly be. This was his mate, and he didn't want to hurt her in any way.

As soon as he slid his teeth in fully and bit, he felt the first part of the bond slide into place. Leah gasped, and he moved his mouth from her shoulder, licking the wound. His wolf prowled inside him, eager to complete the bond yet almost at peace with what had happened. She was a warm part of him for eternity now, and he couldn't wait to finish the bond.

He tilted his head to the side, and she kissed his neck. Though he kept moving in and out of her, he tried not to move too quickly and startle what was happening between them. When she bit down on his shoulder he shuddered, his wolf pressing into him in bliss.

"Fuck, little witch. You're mine," he bit out.

She kissed up his neck then took his mouth. "And you're mine. Now fuck me, my wolf. Make me yours in truth."

He pressed a hard kiss to her mouth then lifted her ass slightly as he angled his thrusts, pumping in and out of her until her breasts bounced and his body ached. She pinched her nipples and licked her lips, smiling as he reached up and cupped her breasts. He couldn't stop touching her, couldn't stop needing her.

When his balls tightened, he lowered himself and kissed her again, not losing his rhythm. "Come for me, little witch. Come around my cock."

He angled his hips just right and her pussy clenched around him. Her eyes rolled to the back of her head and he grinned as she came. When she looked back at him, he pumped hard once more then came.

The mating bond between then clamped shut, a warm burst of lightning and tingles down his spine. He felt her soul. Felt her magic within him. The water in the glass on the counter near them floated into the air and swirled around them, mixing with the magic of the bond between them. The spirits quieted for the first time in longer than he could remember, and he fell to the carpet, rolling and bringing her with him, his cock still deeply inside of her.

"Holy goddess," Ryder whispered.

"That...that was...yeah."

No words, he thought. There were no words. He had his mate in his arms and in his soul. The mating bond flared between them, a pulse of love, passion, and connection he'd never thought possible.

The goddess had blessed him with a woman who not only fought back but also fought for him. Now that he'd given in to the temptation of a future, he knew he'd do whatever it took to keep it.

Leah was his mate, his heart.

And now he'd prove it to her, to him, to everyone.

For eternity.

CHAPTER
THIRTEEN

Once again, Leah found herself standing in front of the Coven, yet this time, she felt no true fear, only anticipation laced with worry. The man that had tried to take her life after giving it to her in the first place lived no longer. The gnawing ache that had once come with the presence of Luis and Darynda was no more.

Ryder hadn't wanted her to come to the Coven meeting with him and the other wolves, though he hadn't voiced as much. She'd felt it through the mating bond. She still couldn't believe they'd mated. It had once seemed like a dream, or at least something so farfetched it would never happen, but now it was reality.

While she understood why Ryder had pushed her away for so long, she also knew it would take longer than an evening of pure passion for her to get over the idea of being left behind because of it. He might not have known what to do with his powers or how they would affect her in the long run, but he hadn't given her a choice in the matter.

She'd forgiven him for it all because she loved him, but she wouldn't forget what had happened anytime soon. If she were to do so, she might forget how hard she'd worked to get where she was, and forget what it had taken to make that happen.

The bond between them flared, and she held back a gasp. She looked to her left at her mate, her mate, and gave him a slight nod. When he reached out and gripped her fingers, she squeezed his hand back. Before, showing any form of attachment would have only painted a target on his back. Now that wasn't the case. The dangers weren't gone completely, not even close, but the main one she had worried about all her life was. Now the idea of a mate, someone who would have her back and cherish her wasn't a burden, but something to be celebrated. She wouldn't have to protect him from her past, but rather, they would protect each other in their future.

Together they were stronger than they ever had been before.

Ryder gave her a slight smile, and the bond pulsated once again. She knew they were in the middle of the mating heat, and if they hadn't needed to meet with the Coven to deal with the Humans First problem, they'd be in bed—or on the floor—right now.

She couldn't wait to get Ryder home and strip him down so she could lick up every inch of him. And boy how many inches that man had in certain places.

Brandon let out a small cough, and Leah blushed. She'd

forgotten the Omega stood to her right. The Omega who could not only scent her arousal but feel her emotions.

As Ryder's mate, she was Pack. She was officially a Talon. She'd been so enraptured with the mating bond and Ryder's body inside hers, she'd completely missed the snap of the Pack bond going into place. When she'd woken from her sex-hazed fog, she'd felt the first stirrings of the Pack bond, as well as those of being the Heir's mate. It would take a while to get used to, but she would. Eventually.

However, that meant she needed to focus on the here and now and focus on whatever the hell was going on between the Pack and the Coven instead of giving Brandon a show with her emotions.

That morning, after a wonderful post-mating shower that had including another bout of mating because, dear goddess, she couldn't keep her hands off of him, Brandon had called to let them know the Coven had requested their presence.

Or rather, what was left of the Coven. As it hadn't been a summons like the previous time the witches had wanted to speak with them, Leah was a little more hopeful on the outcome of this meeting.

The Talons had brought Ryder, Brandon, and herself. The Redwoods had Finn, Drake, Charlotte, and Bram. Charlotte had requested to be there for Leah's sake, and Leah was grateful. Bram, Leah figured, was there for Charlotte. Not that the two looked ready to talk about what the hell was going on with them yet.

And that was how they found themselves, once again, in an older building on neutral ground. They weren't meeting in the previous one, as it had been compromised thanks to Luis. The Coven's numbers had grown since the last time they'd been there, as well, and that was something Leah needed to know more about.

Not all witches were evil, power-hungry, elitist snobs, far from it, but Luis and Darynda hadn't shown that to the Packs.

"Thank you for coming," the pregnant witch finally said. "I'm Amelia, an air witch and the new leader of the Coven." She gave them a self-deprecating smile. "We're in limbo at this point with our leadership."

Ryder tilted his head, looking so much like a wolf she had to hold back a smile of her own. "We're here because the problem hasn't gone away. Humans First, the government, and countless others don't understand our people, and the lack of knowledge leads to dangerous times."

Amelia nodded and looked around at her fellow witches before landing her gaze on Leah. "The Coven has made mistakes. Not all of them were made with the knowledge of the Coven, but we allowed Luis and Darynda to rule us for far too long."

"They threatened our families," another witch said from Amelia's side. He was younger than Luis had been, as were many of the current members in front of Leah.

Amelia's jaw tightened. "We will not allow that to happen again. We are a peaceful people. Do no harm. That is the first rule of being a witch, and yet, some of the former members of the Coven didn't seem to understand that. We might be in the middle of a transition within our own borders, but we know there is more at stake than who rules a coven and what happens within our people."

Ryder nodded. Leah knew the Talons understood this better than anyone. Their change might have happened over a decade ago, but they were still feeling the aftermath of that hierarchy shift. That was what happened when one lived hundreds of years.

"We need to define the narrative," Amelia continued.

"We can try," Leah put in. "But people are so scared right now, they don't know what to listen to. It doesn't help that Washington has been oddly quiet except for that one speech."

Ryder let out a small growl. "To me, that means they're planning something. Or more than one something."

"Agreed," Amelia said, her voice solemn.

For the next few hours, they discussed their plans to protect not only their people but also their future. It wouldn't be easy, and it wouldn't happen overnight. The Talons and Redwoods didn't speak for the entire world of wolves, nor did the Coven for all witches. But they were the main voices in this fight because of where things were percolating. Leah knew there was one wolf, a Redwood named Parker, who was out in the world, meeting with other Packs, and keeping things up-to-date. Technology only went so far. Things were starting to move faster toward a confrontation, and at least a new knowing. Leah would be by Ryder's side for all of it. She refused to stand back and allow the world to change without her. She'd hidden for far too long as it was.

Roland was gone, but his legacy, the idea of a life not on

the run, would not fade. She would live that for him because he never had the chance. She would fight for her people, witches and wolves.

She'd been given this gift and she wouldn't lose it.

Once the meeting ended, the tired group of wolves headed out to their vehicles. They'd made plans for speeches, and how they would continue to try and define their narrative, but in reality, it was only the first step. If the government or Humans First came at them, they would have to be prepared to fight. They'd done their best to not kill anyone who tried to hurt them outside of their circles, but soon that might have to change.

They could only protect their families so much without resorting to a result that would end in blood and tears. That result could hurt their images, but as of now, their image was murky anyway.

Politics and media streams hurt her head, and she wanted to go back to the Pack and worry about something a little more insular than the end of the world as she knew it.

Ryder's arm went around her shoulders as they made their way to their SUV. She leaned in to his hold and inhaled his scent. She couldn't use her nose the way wolves could, but she still loved the smell of him. He settled her in a way she hadn't thought possible before.

Brandon moved past them and shook his head. "Next time I'm bringing Kameron and Mitchell. You two and your mating heat are just about killing me."

Leah bit her lip to keep from laughing, but Ryder had no qualms about chuckling. "You'd rather deal with their icy emotions than our mating?"

Brandon met Ryder's eyes, and Leah had to hold her breath. "Their pain and ice soothes the heat at times." With that, the Omega got into the back of the SUV, and Leah leaned in to her mate.

"Maybe we can tone it down for him."

Ryder kissed her softly then moved back. "Maybe. It's all so new, though, that I don't even realize I'm doing it." He looked over her shoulder and frowned. "Did I give you my tablet?"

She checked her bag and shook her head. "No. Did you leave it in the room?"

Ryder cursed. "Yeah. Fuck. Okay, I'll be right back. Stay in the car." He kissed her once more and jogged back to the building.

Leah let out a breath and got into the passenger seat of the SUV, her eyes on the building.

"You don't have to keep your emotions tamped down around me," Brandon said from behind her. "I'm the Omega, I feel everything. My brother deserves this happiness far more than I can even contemplate. I'd known something was wrong with him, or rather that something was hurting him for years, but I couldn't figure it out. I couldn't help. The fact that your bond seems to have settled him just a little bit makes any oddness I feel worth it and more."

Leah turned in her seat to look at Brandon. She didn't know what she would do if she had to feel every single emotion of the Pack. She could feel the souls of the Pack in her heart as it was, but it was almost muted, as if the goddess were giving her time to figure out how she would help the Talons in the future. However, Brandon, and Gideon for that matter, seemed to have it at full force.

"You're not to blame for Ryder keeping his gift a secret." Ryder had told his family that morning what he'd been hiding all those years. They weren't happy with him, but they'd banded together to make sure he was cared for. For that matter, Leah didn't know how she would help him if the spirits got to be too much, but she'd damn well try. He wasn't alone anymore, and neither was she.

"I wish he'd have told us earlier, but I understand he thought we all needed to have one good memory about our uncles. As well as the fact that he hadn't wanted to bother anyone with his pain. We're all idiots when it comes to protecting one another from our faults." Brandon snorted then stared off into the distance.

She didn't know his secrets, and it wasn't her place to ask him about them, but she'd learn one day what it meant to be part of a family. She was a Talon now—a far greater network than merely her mother and brother.

Brandon stiffened then jumped out of the SUV. She followed him, her body on alert.

"What is it?" she asked quietly.

"I thought I heard a crash." He met Leah's gaze. "And Ryder should have been back by now."

She tripped over a rock and righted herself. Goddess, no. She tried to feel the bond and came up short. She still didn't know how to work with it. It was still so new that sometimes she couldn't find it. It was there, she knew that at least because she hadn't felt it break, but she couldn't find him.

She ran after Brandon, the Redwoods on their tails since they hadn't left yet. If the witches had hurt her mate...she balled her hands into fists, trying to keep her magic under control. They ran into the conference room and came up short.

"He's not here," she whispered.

Ryder's tablet lay on the table, untouched. No one else was in the room; the witches had left the room the same time the wolves had.

"I don't scent anyone," Brandon growled out.

"I don't either," Finn added. "Fuck. Who the hell took Ryder?"

Her body shook and she reached out to grab the tablet. The metal was cold. No one had touched it since they'd left.

"Where is he?" she whispered. Her magic slid through her, ready to fight. But without knowing who to fight, she came up short.

"Finn? Can you come over here?" Charlotte knelt on the floor next to the side door, a frown on her face. "Everyone else keep your distance. I think I scent something, but I don't want to mix it with others."

Leah froze but tried not to be annoyed that she couldn't help. She didn't have the senses the others did, but hopefully, she'd be able to help in some way.

Finn carefully moved toward his cousin and cursed. "It's human. Fucking human."

"It's mixed with Ryder's scent," Charlotte added then moved back to Bram's side.

Leah's knees buckled but she didn't fall. Brandon stood

at her side, looking as if he were ready to catch her, but she couldn't look weak.

"We'll find him," Leah bit out. "We'll find him and make those who took him pay."

Finn met her gaze, his wolf in his eyes. "Hell yeah. They don't fucking take what's ours."

"We'll need to follow the trail," Bram put in. "How's your mating bond?" he asked Leah.

Leah shook her head. "I don't know how to use it, but I'll figure it out."

Because she had to. Someone had taken her mate, her Ryder. And there was no way she'd let that stand. She would find him as he'd found her once before. They were meant for eternity, and she'd be damned if she'd let that eternity end now.

She'd find him.

She had to.

RYDER HELD BACK A SCREAM. The blade slid into his fingertip as if searching for hidden claws. Fucking humans didn't understand that it wasn't an actual wolf right under his skin. It was his wolf, another part of his body and soul. They shared his body, but not at the same time. It was magic.

The man currently slicing off parts of Ryder's skin couldn't just peel it all away to see his wolf. The goddess had both blessed and cursed them with the magic of their wolves.

Humans would never truly understand, and yet this one

wanted to find an analytical and sadistic way to prove that magic truly existed.

Ryder had been a fucking idiot. Seriously. He hadn't even scented the damn humans until it was too late. He'd gone inside for his tablet and had ended up with four darts in his body. He'd moved fast enough to duck another ten of them, but the humans after him had been prepared.

If he'd been a weaker wolf, he might have died from the amount of drugs coursing through his system. They'd knocked him out and dragged him to whatever building they held him in now. Though his body raged in agony at the slices on his skin and the drugs in his veins, his wolf was at the front, taking in every detail of the place he could.

He was underground in a bunker of some sort, but this was no hovel, it was some high-end expanse. Large cages lined the walls, though they were empty. He didn't want to know why they were empty. He wouldn't be able to take it. Bright lights covered the room, bathing it in a sickly glow, and long medical beds dotted the area. The thick belts and leather cuffs attached to each bed weren't lost on him.

He wasn't in a place designed to help people. He was in a place where people were studied. Vivisected. Murdered.

He needed to get the fuck out.

"He's bleeding like the others, but he seems to have a firmer spine," the butcher in front of him stated coldly.

Ryder let out a growl, just a slight warning before looking over the man's shoulder at the familiar face in the doorway.

Senator McMaster.

The eagle-eyed, smooth talking politician, who had

been the first in power to speak out against the supernatural. The man had subtlety put a firm boundary between humans and those who were not. The Pack had been keeping an eye on him, but it seemed they had missed something crucial.

The man had plans of his own.

"You wolves think you're the top predator, the top of the food chain, yet you've spent the past year hiding, waiting." McMaster slowly moved toward Ryder, even as the butcher with the knife kept cutting.

The slices burned, and blood flowed from his body, but the man with the knife knew what he was doing. Ryder wouldn't die from the cuts, but he'd hurt until he did something stupid—like give up key information about his Pack.

That meant Ryder would have to do his best to keep that from happening. No matter the pain. It killed him that he couldn't feel Leah like he should. The drugs and searing agony made his mind a little muddled—enough that he was having a hard time finding the bond and keeping track of where she was or what she was feeling. Their bond was too new, too fragile. If they'd been mated for years like the Redwoods were, maybe Leah and the Talons would have had a chance to find him.

As it was, he was afraid it would be too late.

He'd die with his secrets, die for his Pack, but he'd be damned if he went easily.

"It was really quite exhilarating seeing you change on the screen as you did," McMaster continued. He gestured toward the empty cages. "The ones that came before you shifted countless times for me, but they didn't have the same...finesse that you had when you were jumping through fire for that witch."

Ryder's wolf held back a whimper at the idea of so many lost wolves. He knew they hadn't been Talons or Redwoods since there hadn't been any disappearances, but they could have been Centrals, lone wolves, or countless others. He couldn't let them die in vain.

"What do you think is so special about me?" he bit out. His fangs threatened to slide through his gums and he inhaled deeply. He couldn't afford to lose control.

"I think you're much more special than you allow others to see, Heir of the Talons."

Ryder bit back a curse. They fucking knew too much. They always had.

"I'm going to see what you look like on the inside, wolf. I want to see what makes you tick. The Humans First movement helps my cause, as does Washington's inadequacies, but soon, you will know what I want. And before you can do anything about it, you'll die drowning in your own blood." McMaster turned to his butcher. "Keep going. I want to see him bleed."

With that, the politician with the cool smile left him alone with the monster that didn't scare him as much as McMaster himself.

Ryder met the man's eyes and refused to scream, refused to growl. They would not win. He might die at their hands, but he wouldn't lose his pride.

Time seemed to drag on as the man made his cuts. They almost didn't hurt anymore and that worried him. Ryder pulled at his restraints, but that only made the monster cut deeper. There was no way he would escape this, not without help. He couldn't sense his mate, his Pack, but if he inhaled deeply enough, he could have sworn he was able to scent them.

Perhaps this was it. This was his death.

He'd never have Leah in his arms again; never see her grow round with his child.

His wolf pushed at him, begging him to hold on, to wait for a time where they could break free. Ryder didn't give in to the part of his soul that had grown tired; he fought, even if that meant staying where he was.

He was wolf. He was Talon. He was Heir.

He would try to survive because he needed his Leah.

The door opened, and Ryder tried to lift his head, only to find it too heavy. Thick boots sounded on the floor as someone came forward. Ryder couldn't tell who it was, but he prayed to the goddess it was a way out.

He'd fought all his life to keep his mind sane and his body whole, and now it seemed that a human would be the one to best him. He couldn't give up...he wouldn't.

The butcher didn't look over his shoulder, but Ryder didn't give anything away. He might not recognize the soldier behind the butcher, but from the way the soldier moved, Ryder didn't want to halt his plan.

The soldier in front of him, garbed head to toe in a black uniform with no insignia, took the man by the back of the neck and pulled him away from Ryder. With a few quick movements, the other man was knocked out and tied up within a cage.

"We don't have a lot of time," the soldier said quietly as he worked to get Ryder free.

"Why are you helping me?" Ryder bit out as he tried not to growl. He stood on shaky legs, refusing to put his weight on the other man.

"I joined the military to serve my country, then when I got out, I joined this group to keep our people safe. That's not what's going on." He didn't say anything else but gave Ryder a look. "They'll know I was here soon if we don't get out of here quickly."

"What's your name?" Ryder asked.

"Shane." He didn't give a last name and Ryder narrowed his eyes.

"You were there the day of the Unveiling. You were the one who helped Brynn."

Shane raised his chin. "We need to go." He didn't confirm or deny what Ryder had said, but Ryder recognized the man.

His body shook and his cuts burned, but he followed the man out the door. His wolf didn't trust Shane fully, but he had a feeling this was the way to go.

With each step, he knew he was getting to Leah, and that was all that mattered.

For now.

SHANE

Shane was a fucking idiot. He'd betrayed his country, his team, to save this one wolf. But if he hadn't, he'd have kept the dark mark on his soul for far longer than he could live with. As it was, he'd only just found out about the true natures of McMaster and Montag.

Now, he'd taken a stance with this Ryder, but no one on his team actually knew what he'd done. He'd disabled the cameras and hid his tracks, but if he weren't careful, he wouldn't live long enough to find a way to right the wrongs of those he'd once trusted.

"I can get you to the outside of the compound, but then I need to go back," Shane said softly, careful of who might overhear. "I can't let them know I've gone rogue."

Ryder met his gaze. "You want to gather more information. Work from the inside."

Shane nodded once. He would do what he could with the time he had left. If the public knew exactly what went on inside these walls...hell, he couldn't even think of the ramifications.

"Come to us," Ryder said finally. "Come to us when you need to. My wolf trusts you, though I don't know why."

Shane let out a breath and continued to move. He knew shifters weren't the bringers of death the others thought, but he didn't know if he could give up everything to live with them like that. He also didn't know if he could truly trust them, knowing what he'd been part of in the past.

All he knew was that he had to get Ryder to safety and hurry back before it was too late. As soon as he got to the edge of the perimeter, he froze. Someone else was out there. He could feel it. He might only be human, but he was far more trained than most.

Ryder let out a slight growl. "My people are close. They must have followed my scent." There was something else left unsaid, Shane could tell, but he didn't have time to figure out this wolf's secrets.

"Ryder!" A light-brown-haired woman came toward them, her palms out and water sliding over them.

A witch, then. The same one from the feed that had shown Ryder change from man to wolf.

"I'm here. Shane got me out."

Others slid from the trees, but he knew there were more than just those who had shown themselves. Wolves were pack hunters, after all.

Shane stood back and waited for the witch to hold Ryder close. Two males came forward and helped Ryder move, their feet not making a sound. Shane watched all of this with a careful eye, but it was the dark-haired beauty that captured most of his attention.

He didn't know who she was, nor why he couldn't stop staring, but she looked right back at him. Her eyes narrowed and she turned away. A dark-skinned man glared at him and then followed her.

"I need to go back before they notice I'm gone," Shane finally said.

Ryder looked over his shoulder. "You can come with us," he said honestly.

Shane shook his head. "If we all go, how we will know who the monsters are?" With one last look at the woman, he trotted back toward the compound.

He made his way into the building without making a sound, his thoughts going in a thousand different directions. It was probably for that reason that he didn't hear the sound of the gun going off until it was too late, or feel the burn at his side until his head hit the floor.

He'd been found.

It was too late.

And yet, all he could think of was the woman with the honey-colored eyes and the man who had been behind her.

A stark image to have as one's last impression, even in the throes of death.

CHAPTER
FOURTEEN

L eah tried to keep from crying as she and Charlotte bandaged up Ryder's wounds. There was no use, though, because she was just so damned grateful for the human who had saved his life. Her mate had almost died, and she'd almost been too late to stop it.

The SUV hit another rut, and she banged her head on the ceiling. Holding back a curse, she glared up at Brandon.

"Sorry. I'm trying to go as fast as we can so we can get to Walker and behind the wards. We're off-roading as it is."

She let out a sigh and went back to cleaning up her mate. Only the fact that Ryder needed help held Leah back from snarling at Charlotte for daring to touch her mate's skin. She might not be a wolf, but, apparently, she had mating territorial issues.

As soon as they'd caught Ryder's scent back at the Coven meeting place, they'd all jumped into one SUV and did their best to follow it. Between that and the low pulse of the mating bond she'd finally been able to find, they'd found where the humans were keeping Ryder.

It had only been by chance that they'd gotten there when Shane showed with Ryder leaning heavily on him. She didn't know anything about the human, other than the fact that he'd saved her mate's life. She would be forever grateful for the man's actions, even if she didn't fully understand them.

They worked on Ryder's wounds in silence, though he kept his hand on her thigh. Some cuts were too deep for what little first aid they could do on the move, but the others would heal on their own as soon as he shifted and got some protein in his system. Walker would have to work on the rest. But at least they could stop most of the bleeding.

She knew she'd almost lost him because of the amount of cuts on his body. How her brave mate could sit there and not growl or whimper was beyond her.

"I'm getting blood all over my seats," Ryder said softly.

She kissed his cheek where they'd already cleaned up the blood. "It can be cleaned. If not, then, whatever. You're here to bleed on them, and that's all that matters."

"That's my mate, always looking on the bright side," Ryder said sleepily.

"Don't go to sleep yet, darling," she put in. "Not until you have Walker check you out."

"I'm here with you," Ryder whispered. "That's all that matters."

"And the rest of us are just chopped liver," Drake said from the back of the SUV. He, Brandon, and Bram knelt together, not looking too comfortable in the small, enclosed space.

"True," Charlotte said with a smile. "We're not Leah. But we're here for you anyway." She handed Ryder some beef jerky. "Now eat this before you pass out. Your wolf is hungry."

He took it from her and chewed as Leah worked on a deep cut on his side. Each wound tugged at her and the mating bond flared. But when she looked into Ryder's eyes, she knew it would be okay. At least for now. It surprised her how quickly she'd fallen for him, even with how hard they'd tried to stay apart. And yet, she knew this was exactly where she should be. At his side, no matter the pain, no matter the cost.

By the time they got to the Talon den and Walker had Healed him as much as he could, Ryder looked exhausted and ready to pass out. Thankfully, they were allowed to go back to his place—their place now—so he could rest.

There would be time for talking, planning, and dealing with the ramifications of what Ryder had witnessed, but first, her mate needed to Heal. Kameron and Mitchell were on their way back to the compound to see what information they could gather; however, Leah wanted to focus on Ryder first. The other worries could wait.

Walker had helped strip Ryder and put him in bed, leaving Leah to tend to him for now. While her mate slept, she quickly showered, washing his blood from her skin and soaking in the water, needing its healing presence to soothe her soul as well as her body.

She'd almost lost him today, and she hadn't even had

the chance to fully take action against those who took him. One day soon she would, she knew, but for now, just having Ryder near would have to be enough. Her Pack and her new family were in danger, and all she wanted to do was cuddle into her mate and try to remember that there was a reason they fought.

That, in its own way, was another form of healing. One she needed to embrace.

She shut off the water and dried herself off before walking naked into the bedroom. Ryder slept on his back, his wounds almost fully healed. Because he hadn't broken any bones nor hurt any internal organs, he'd be back to full strength by the morning. It should have surprised her, but considering what she could do with her own magic, it didn't.

Leah lifted the covers and slid into the bed beside him, careful not to jostle his nearly healed wounds. When he turned his head and opened his eyes, she bit her lip, another tear sliding down her cheek.

"Never do that again." Her voice broke. "I can't stand the thought of losing you."

He lifted his arm, and she carefully pressed her naked body to his. Immediately, her magic reached out and wrapped around him, needing him as much as his wolf needed her. The bond pulsed red-hot between them, and she sighed.

"I'm sorry, little witch. The only thing I thought about when I was there was seeing you again. I don't know what I'd do without you." He kissed her forehead and she sighed.

"I love you, Leah. You're my mate, my heart, the other half of my soul. I love you."

The tears flowed freely down her cheeks now. "I love you, too, my wolf."

They'd mated already, and the bond between them glowed brightly. But it was the words that the humans needed.

Together, they lay cuddled under the blankets, healing in a way that only they would understand. They'd fought together and had saved one another from not only the outside world but also the demons within.

When she'd been running for her life, she'd never thought to find the one person who could complete her in a way that never left her wanting. And yet, the goddess had blessed her with not only a mate, but a male who truly understood what she could provide to the Pack.

She would fight by his side and fight for their Pack. She was witch, she was Talon, she was Ryder's. And most of all, she was Leah.

She wasn't alone anymore.

Not by far.

EPILOGUE

Ryder gripped his mate's hips, pumping in and out of her as they both panted with need. Leah knelt in front of him, her hands fisting in the sheets as he fucked her from behind. With one hand, he slid his fingers over her and probed her ass. When she gasped and pushed back, he slowly worked his way inside, his fingers slick from her juices.

That movement made her come, her pussy clenching around his dick. Since he couldn't hold back when he was with her, he thrust into her once more then came, as well, filling her up until they both lay together on the bed, spent and sweaty.

"Good morning," Leah panted.

"Good morning," Ryder chuckled. He kissed her neck then slid slowly out of her. "We need to shower if we're going to make it to Brie and Gideon's on time."

As a former member of the Redwood Pack, Brie had been used to family dinners. The Brentwoods, it seemed, were now having weekly meals at their place. Ryder couldn't find fault in the idea, other than the fact that it meant he had to get dressed and out of bed. But now that the others knew what he could do and what Leah would soon learn to do with her share of his craft, he didn't want to hide from them anymore. Family meant getting the good and the bad, and he had to remember that. They had always been there for him, and he would always be there for them in turn.

Leah spooned back into him and grinned over her shoulder. "Brie is making a roast. Let's get dressed."

He smacked her ass then rubbed the sting. "You're trading me in for a roast?"

She turned in his arms, gripped his dick and kissed his lips. "I need fuel so I can keep riding you long into the night. Roast first. Hot sex later."

He laughed before kissing her again. "Deal."

They showered quickly and made sure every inch of each other was clean before getting dressed and ready to head out. Leah grabbed the deviled eggs she'd made earlier and handed them over to him.

"You're the big, strong wolf. You can carry these."

He just shrugged and did as he was told like a good mate. It didn't make much sense to argue.

Though they were still on the hunt for those who could hurt their Pack and worried about the repercussions of what Ryder had learned while in captivity, they couldn't forget that their Pack and family needed emotional health, as well. The compound had been deserted when Kameron and Mitchell went back. The fact that it had emptied so quickly worried Ryder. That meant there was more than one place McMaster and his staff could hide.

That also meant that Shane was nowhere to be found.

The man had saved Ryder's life and the lives of his mate and Packmates. Without Shane, the others would have had to fight to get inside the compound and back out again. He hoped Shane was alive somewhere, but he couldn't be sure. Not anymore.

The witches were quiet, but ready to keep their side of the treaty intact. He would be forever grateful for Leah and the way she worked with Amelia. The witches and wolves were out in the public eye now. And, like they had said before, they were the ones who needed to keep the narrative threaded with truth. Ryder just hoped it was still an option.

They were fighting an unseen enemy from so many sides, it made Ryder's head ache. But as long as he remembered that he wasn't alone anymore, he could do it.

You're alone, boy. You just keep forgetting it.

He didn't wince at his uncle's words. Didn't acknowledge them.

Leah, however, narrowed her eyes and flicked her hand in the air. Mist surrounded them, and his uncle's voice faded away.

Ryder just smiled at his mate; relieved that she was learning how to deal with her new powers. She couldn't control the spirits, nor could Ryder. But they were working together to not be afraid of them. As for his uncle, well, they were learning to make the asshole go away so he wouldn't torture Ryder anymore. Maybe one day soon they'd learn to get rid of him in truth, but first, they had a family dinner to attend.

One thing at a time, he reminded himself. One day at a time.

As they made their way to Gideon's house, Ryder's phone chirped. Leah gave him a questioning glance and he checked the screen, only to frown.

"I need to go to the front gates," he said slowly. "There's someone there who is asking for me."

Leah's eyebrows shot up. "Seriously?"

He nodded. It was unusual, as humans couldn't actually see the wards nor the den, though they tried. That meant whoever it was had to be at least part supernatural. Maybe. Things were changing daily so he really didn't know anymore.

"Do you want to go on to the house?" he asked, knowing the answer before he'd even asked the question.

She just raised her brow and took the eggs from him. "Keep your claws ready, wolf boy."

With that, he kissed her forehead and they made their way to the gates. As soon as he caught sight of who stood there, he broke out into a run. He heard Leah set the eggs down on the ground and follow him, her legs pumping as fast as she could.

"Shane?" he called out.

The human stood—barely—and raised his chin. Sweat

poured down his face and he looked as if he'd been through hell and back.

"I need your help, Ryder," the human panted. With that, Shane fell to the ground, his head slamming into the dirt.

Ryder cursed and pushed through the wards, going to his knees to check Shane's pulse. It beat rapidly, and the man's skin was cool and clammy. There was a gunshot wound on his side, but from the scent, someone had patched him up.

However, that wasn't the only thing in the man's scent. A tang he couldn't quite place was mixed with the human scent Shane had held before. Something had happened to him, something bad.

His wolf went on alert, ready to see if this were a trap, but he had a feeling Shane was on his own.

"Dear goddess, what's wrong with him?" Leah asked.

Ryder met her gaze and saw the worry etched on her face. "I think he's dying. I...I don't know what to do. He's not Pack."

Gideon was suddenly there, his hands balled into fists. "This is the man that saved you?" his brother, his Alpha asked.

Ryder nodded. "Yes, but there's something off about his scent."

Gideon cursed. "The moon goddess spoke to me, that's why I'm here. I got here as fast as I could. She told me to bring him into the Pack." He met Ryder's eyes. "If I do this, we could bring more trouble to our borders."

Ryder looked down at the man who had saved his life.

Had saved Brynn's life. The moon goddess rarely spoke directly to wolves. If she had done so, it was important. Far more important than he realized he was sure. "We already have trouble, Gideon. A whole shitload."

With that, Gideon cursed and let his claws out. He slashed his palm, then Shane's, before slamming them together. The Alpha's power pulsed outward, and Leah went to her knees beside Ryder. With one hand on Shane, Ryder wrapped the other arm around his mate.

"It is done," Gideon growled. "He is Pack. Now Walker can Heal him and we can see what the fuck is going on."

The Pack bonds fluctuated and Ryder's eyes widened as he felt Shane's bonds tie to his as Heir.

"Holy shit," Ryder breathed.

Leah tugged on his hand. "What is it?"

"He's wolf but not," Gideon growled out. "How the fuck did that happen?"

"He's not fully wolf," Ryder whispered. "He's...something different." He met his Alpha's gaze. "What the fuck did the humans do?"

Leah turned in his arms and forced his gaze to hers. "Dear goddess..."

He looked down at his mate, then down at the man who had saved his life and yet might be the one thing to bring chaos to his Pack.

The world had shifted once again, and Ryder stood at the precipice, waiting for a resolution. He had his mate, he had his powers, he had his Pack. That would have to be enough. Because if it wasn't, the Talons were lost.

Again.

THE END

Next in the Talon Pack World...
Its Charlotte's turn in Wolf Betrayed.

A NOTE FROM CARRIE ANN

Thank you so much for reading Mated in Mist! I do hope if you liked this story, that you would please leave a review! Reviews help authors and readers.

If you want to make sure you know what's coming next from me, you can sign up for my newsletter at www.CarrieAnnRyan.com; follow me on twitter at @CarrieAnnRyan, or like my Facebook page. I also have a Facebook Fan Club where we have trivia, chats, and other goodies. You guys are the reason I get to do what I do and I thank you.

Make sure you're signed up for my MAILING LIST so you can know when the next releases are available as well as find giveaways and FREE READS.

Happy Reading!

The Talon Pack:
Book 1: Tattered Loyalties
Book 2: An Alpha's Choice

ABOUT THE AUTHOR

Carrie Ann Ryan is the New York Times and USA Today bestselling author of contemporary, paranormal, and young adult romance. Her works include the Montgomery Ink, Redwood Pack, Fractured Connections, and Elements of Five series, which have sold over 3.0 million books worldwide. She started writing while in graduate school for her advanced degree in chemistry and hasn't stopped since. Carrie Ann has written over seventy-five novels and novellas with more in the works. When she's not losing herself in her emotional and action-packed worlds, she's reading as much as she can while wrangling her clowder of cats who have more followers than she does.

www.CarrieAnnRyan.com

ALSO FROM THIS AUTHOR

Book 2: From Flame and Ash
Book 3: From Spirit and Binding
Book 4: From Shadow and Silence

The Promise Me Series:
Book 1: Forever Only Once
Book 2: From That Moment
Book 3: Far From Destined
Book 4: From Our First

The Fractured Connections Series:
Book 1: Breaking Without You
Book 2: Shouldn't Have You
Book 3: Falling With You
Book 4: Taken With You

Montgomery Ink: Colorado Springs
Book 1: Fallen Ink
Book 2: Restless Ink
Book 2.5: Ashes to Ink
Book 3: Jagged Ink
Book 3.5: Ink by Numbers

Montgomery Ink:
Book 0.5: Ink Inspired
Book 0.6: Ink Reunited
Book 1: Delicate Ink
Book 1.5: Forever Ink
Book 2: Tempting Boundaries
Book 3: Harder than Words

Book 4: Written in Ink
Book 4.5: Hidden Ink
Book 5: Ink Enduring
Book 6: Ink Exposed
Book 6.5: Adoring Ink
Book 6.6: Love, Honor, & Ink
Book 7: Inked Expressions
Book 7.3: Dropout
Book 7.5: Executive Ink
Book 8: Inked Memories
Book 8.5: Inked Nights
Book 8.7: Second Chance Ink

The Gallagher Brothers Series:
Book 1: Love Restored
Book 2: Passion Restored
Book 3: Hope Restored

The Whiskey and Lies Series:
Book 1: Whiskey Secrets
Book 2: Whiskey Reveals
Book 3: Whiskey Undone

The Talon Pack:
Book 1: Tattered Loyalties
Book 2: An Alpha's Choice
Book 3: Mated in Mist
Book 4: Wolf Betrayed
Book 5: Fractured Silence
Book 6: Destiny Disgraced

ALSO FROM THIS AUTHOR

Book 7: Eternal Mourning
Book 8: Strength Enduring
Book 9: Forever Broken

Redwood Pack Series:
Book 1: An Alpha's Path
Book 2: A Taste for a Mate
Book 3: Trinity Bound
Book 3.5: A Night Away
Book 4: Enforcer's Redemption
Book 4.5: Blurred Expectations
Book 4.7: Forgiveness
Book 5: Shattered Emotions
Book 6: Hidden Destiny
Book 6.5: A Beta's Haven
Book 7: Fighting Fate
Book 7.5: Loving the Omega
Book 7.7: The Hunted Heart
Book 8: Wicked Wolf

The Branded Pack Series:
(Written with Alexandra Ivy)
Book 1: Stolen and Forgiven
Book 2: Abandoned and Unseen
Book 3: Buried and Shadowed

Dante's Circle Series:
Book 1: Dust of My Wings
Book 2: Her Warriors' Three Wishes
Book 3: An Unlucky Moon

Book 3.5: His Choice
Book 4: Tangled Innocence
Book 5: Fierce Enchantment
Book 6: An Immortal's Song
Book 7: Prowled Darkness
Book 8: Dante's Circle Reborn

Holiday, Montana Series:
Book 1: Charmed Spirits
Book 2: Santa's Executive
Book 3: Finding Abigail
Book 4: Her Lucky Love
Book 5: Dreams of Ivory

The Happy Ever After Series:
Flame and Ink
Ink Ever After

Single Title:
Finally Found You